The Wishing of the Well

Hope in Troubled Waters

By Jonathan Keith Norris

Copyright © 2025

by

Jonathan Keith Norris

All rights reserved. No part of this publication may be reproduced, distributed, or transmitted in any format or by any means, including photocopying, recording, digital sharing, or any electronic method, without the written permission of the publisher on behalf and upon approval of the author, except in the case of brief quotations used in reviews or other permitted noncommercial use under applicable copyright law.

Contents

Dedication: 1
Prologue 2
Chapter 1 - I Do Not Know How I Came to Be 3
Chapter 2 - Out of My Control 10
Chapter 3 - Hope for Desperate Times 15
Chapter 4 - The Great Plot Against Ram the Perpetual 30
Chapter 5 - Man and the Treacherous Steward Meet 41
Chapter 6 - Reason and Mission of the Why 53
Chapter 7 - Cave Number Seven 59
Chapter 8 - The Song of the Mynerts 70
Chapter 9 - The Great Waterfall 81
Chapter 10 - The Cathedral of Myrobah 87
Chapter 11 - Expedition for the Council of Magistrates 100
Chapter 12 - What Awaited Them There 108
Chapter 13 - Hearing Before the House of Magistrates 119
Chapter 14 - The Book and the Amulet 140
Chapter 15 - White Sand and Gold 155
Chapter 16 - The Wish of the Well 167

Dedication:

This book is dedicated to my family and friends. Special loving and grateful thanks I give to my daughter, Chelsea, who inspired me to write this story.

Prologue

"Before all that was known by us, and before all the universe existed, was the great and ever-present mystery W*hy*. This all-encompassing personality of truth and perpetual power was without the reliance of any other substance or thing. The personhood of the *Why* was and is always one with the personhood of the *Reason,* being fulfilled in the personhood of the *Mission.*" So spoke the sage Pondurious to the wide-eyed young man seeking answers, Darius.

The Wishing of the Well unfolds through the eyes of an unlikely narrator: an artesian well. Though a geological feature, this ancient entity possesses thought, memory, and emotion. Free from human prejudice, the well observes with childlike wonder and quiet wisdom, bearing witness to the unfolding drama of humanity.

Its story begins with purity—crystal waters sought by many. But a devastating event poisons its depths, leaving the well broken and the town desperate. When all human efforts fail to restore what was lost, a most unexpected figure emerges: a sage with a tale so mysterious and profound, he claims it as historical truth.

This allegorical journey explores the human condition, the limits of reason, and the enduring power of faith. _The Wishing of the Well_ is based on a timeless story—one that offers hope and healing in the most unlikely of places, when all else seems lost.

Chapter 1 - I Do Not Know How I Came to Be

I am the Well, placed and established with precision and care. Much history lies beneath and around me. I cannot tell you why, when, or how I came to be, but I know I exist to serve all around me which has life. My water once laid above me as a small, overflowing pond, cutting a thin stream down the hill below me. The stream dispersed my water to the trees and plants so they could remain green and grow in the sunlight. The animals sipped from me when they needed to restore their strength. Humans, who are also animals, need me. Over many years, I have gotten to know humans. They can demonstrate great works of beauty, wonder, and goodness. But I have also seen them commit dark and ugly acts, which, unlike the actions of the other animals, seem to have no reason or purpose.

My first introduction to the human animal was when I was discovered by a small group of them dressed in clothing that made it hard to see them in the forest. They were all holding in their hands a strange-looking wooden stick, bent to form an arch by a leather lace tightly strung from one end to the other. Each of them also had a pack, held to their backs by shoulder straps, filled with narrow wooden dowels that had what appeared to be feathers on the tips and sharp, barb-like points on the other ends.

On that day, I first met them; there was a beautiful family of three non-human animals placidly gathering around the mirror pond formed by my water. The sun was shining through the trees. It warmed the open area surrounding my water, making beautiful light refractions formed by leaves and tiny water insects entering and leaving. The family of animals was gathered at my pond's edge peacefully, being refreshed by my cool water. I remember the beautiful circular reflection ripples that intersected each other as each of the grand and gracious beasts' lips touched the water's surface above me. One of them was larger than the others and had emerging out of its head what appeared to be a very small, barren tree. It adorned the beast like a magnificent crown. The crowned placid beast stood watch while the other two took turns timidly and gently sipping from me. They were smaller and had no trees growing out of their heads. The smallest had white spots on its red-brown fur-covered skin. It was a beautiful sight, which filled me with contentment, joy, and peace.

Out of nowhere, I heard a sound like a quick wisp of air coming from one end of my pond. In an instant, it traveled across my water, ending with a sound like a small rock hitting the mossy dirt bank on the other side. The dark and dull impact noise caught my attention from the area where the magnificent creatures drank from me. The one smaller animal without the spots collapsed and fell with its head lying still in my water. One of the narrow rods with feathers on the end of it was now embedded in the shoulder of this beautiful animal. It was motionless while thick red liquid began to rush into me from the object's mark. The liquid had the mineral flavor of iron that I was familiar with. I had often tasted it from the rocks and soil that contained me but had never experienced it from this red, murky, billowing cloud now pouring from the motionless animal. I came to know later that this thick red liquid is what humans call "blood." The remaining animals instantly became frightened and quickly began to run away, disappearing into the surrounding woods.

"Nathan, you fool!" said one approaching human to the other. Two humans appeared out of the woods, racing towards me and the collapsed animal, its shoulder bleeding in my water. One of them had smoke-colored hair and rough-textured skin. He had spoken to the other, whose skin was very smooth and hair the color of burnt trees after a forest fire. "You killed the mother and not the buck. The fawn has not weaned itself from its mother. Have I taught you nothing?"

Catching his breath, the human called Nathan replied, "I'm sorry, Thomas, it was an accident. My aim slipped and I missed my mark."

"You do realize the fawn may not survive without its mother? What a sad loss that would be," said the human called Thomas.

Nathan replied, "Yes, Thomas, I know. I regret my mistake."

Then two other humans burst into the open area from the forest. Both slowed down and came to a sudden stop while they evaluated the situation before them. They each had smooth skin with vibrant hair that differed in color. One had hair the color of the dry field grass surrounding my water's edge. The other had hair the color of the clay which formed my pond's shape. One of them spoke, still breathing heavily, "What happened here, Thomas?"

Without delay, the other chimed in, as if quick to conclude what had happened. "Can't you see with your own eyes, Femi? Nathan missed his mark, as usual."

Nathan, whose tone of voice sounded agitated, retorted, "Exaggerating again, Peter? At least we have something to bring back to the others!" The human called Peter looked at the other called Femi, rolling his eyes while wagging his head; he had nothing more to say.

Then Thomas said, "Nathan is right. Even though it is unfortunate that he made a mistake, we do have food to bring back to our families. Thank you, Nathan. She is a beautiful deer, and her sacrifice was not in vain."

That was when I discovered that these human animals called each other by unique names but called the nonhuman animals by their type. The family of animals that were so peaceful and beautiful was called "deer" by the humans. It was a mystery to me that they would prey on animals that seemed very peaceful, beautiful, and undeserving of such a disturbing fate. They certainly had other choices for food that were non-animal. But for some reason, not known to me at that time, they also needed the flesh of animals to survive.

When all the commotion and exchange of words had settled, they prepared the deer for travel. They tied together its front legs and back legs, then inserted a branch between them, creating a hanger for two of the humans to carry it from both sides. But before they left, preparing to take turns to carry it away, the human called Nathan approached me to draw some water with his cupped hands. He was obviously very thirsty after the strenuous effort it took to kill and prepare the deer for travel back home. By now, the blood from the dead beast had dispersed by the current of the stream flowing out of my pond. As Nathan drew the water from me and tasted it, his eyes grew wide, and he said to the others, "My word, this is some of the best-tasting and cleanest water I have ever experienced! Come, Thomas, and refresh yourself before we return." Thomas and the others stopped what they were doing to approach my water's edge. They had clearly all been caught up in the task at hand and didn't notice how thirsty they were. The others began to drink from me with surprised and satisfied expressions on their faces.

"Well, Nathan," the human named Peter said, "at least you got this right."

Soon after that first experience with those humans and the family of deer, other humans came to visit me. They decided they should build walls around my opening and create a spot where anyone could bring a container and lower it down to collect from me. Time passed, days turned to years, and all the while, more and more humans would come to draw from me. I remember there were times they would become impatient or require more water. They would fight and quarrel, but usually one of them would convince the others to be patient and wait their turn.

As more and more humans visited, drawing water from me, I could see the area around me beginning to change. Small structures were built for farming, food, supplies, and homes for humans. More and more of the structures seemed to appear and occupy the area surrounding me. The farmers needed water from me for the plants, which provided food for them. The builders needed my water to provide moisture for mortar and bricks.

Time continued, and soon a small town was developed with a governing body and many other humans. The governing body and other solicited human experts advised the town that it was time to use modern construction to provide an elaborate means by which to distribute my water more efficiently and abundantly. This would be a system that could deliver my water to many areas of the town by pipes, pumps, filters, tanks, and valves. A very elaborate and complicated water plant was commissioned by human researchers and developers. They had all confirmed my location was over an area where fresh water flowed deep beneath me. It was also revealed through research and science that the water source was plentiful, clean, and endless. They gave me a name to classify my nature and said I was an artesian well. Many more humans would be revived and refreshed by my supply of clean and life-sustaining refreshment. Much industry would be supplied and supported, and farming would yield food far more plentifully and efficiently.

The great filtration plant over me stood proudly in a prominent location on the hill of the town, like a mighty monument. It was truly a crowning accomplishment of modern design and engineering. It took three years to complete the plant, and at least three more following to provide all the connection points that currently exist. The uniqueness of the assembly of structures and towers, all connected by huge pipes painted bright blue, exhibiting an intricate complexity of lines, makes it a very impressive display for all to behold. The humans who pass by gather in front of me during their breaks or while touring the area and praise me with pride as a crown of human accomplishment. The outer perimeter of the plant offers a large, brick-paved courtyard and a central platform gazebo. The gazebo and courtyard are often used for outdoor performances and meetings. This dedicated area is adorned by a beautiful arboretum of foliage with arranged gardens surrounded by park benches and lovely walkways. All was provided by the human town's government for the use and enjoyment of all who lived in the township. I often wonder if they overlook the most important thing, the water I give. This was not made by human hands.

Chapter 2 - Out of My Control

No human could have ever known the tragic disaster that awaited me. One day, there was a geological disturbance, and magnanimous deposits of caustic materials were shifted in the direction of my source. This made my oasis of refreshing water a toxic potion. The methods used to treat my water were overwhelmed by the endless contamination. I cannot tell you why this occurred since it was an event which happened far outside my fixed view. The human researchers and developers jumped to conclusions and began to accuse others of sabotage, rounding up suspects for the crime of vandalism. Not knowing at that point what had happened, I was also quick to blame and side with them. I began to believe the humans I existed to help were hostile and unappreciative of my goodness. Were they seeking some kind of revenge because of spite and jealousy, destroying my purpose? What had I done other than provide hydration and health to them all? I refused to believe it was just an accident.

Rorke, one of the research and development teamsman, was carrying a ledger that contained the names of other humans who were suspected of tampering with me. Mannion, one of the plant workers, was busy taking notes and monitoring my water condition when Rorke approached him. Rorke called out to Mannion to meet privately outside the plant. "We have studied the log sheets at the plant, and they show you checked in on the day the well water was discovered to be contaminated. However, an associate of yours claims he never saw you that day. Where were you and why were you not at your post?"

Mannion, looking annoyed and indignant for being held suspect, replied. "I wasn't at work that day, Rorke."

"But the log sheets show you to be at work. Are you lying to me, Mannion?" Rorke questioned.

Mannion wasn't having any of this blame-quest interrogation nonsense. "Maybe you should ask Hanon. That indolent sloth has a habit of pre-entering information into the logs if he wants to nick some time for his so-called *personal interest*. This makes him the liar, not me. Perhaps you need to take a closer look at him. But laying all accusations aside, Rorke, if you knew anything about the size of the contamination, you wouldn't be looking to blame just one person. It seems to me this would have taken a coordinated effort by many, not just one or two people."

Rorke snapped back at the plant worker, "If you are so sure of yourself, Mannion, then perhaps you should contact public relations to apply for my position. You seem to be implying I don't know what I am doing."

I was growing weary, annoyed, and impatient with the petty back-and-forth of the two humans and their irrelevant turf war of blame and ego. I was becoming sicker, and my restoration was critical. The humans who loved me for my glorious water, who would at times gather before me in the courtyard in front of the plant with grateful admiration, were now at a loss and accusing one another of foul play out of desperation.

Mannion, realizing that Rorke was just desperate to give the mayor and his staff some answers, lowered his defenses. With a more consoling tone, he replied, "Look, I know you are frustrated, and you and the others in your department have been working hard to get to the bottom of this. If you really want my opinion, it is time to consult with the science department for answers. It's difficult for me to believe anyone could have had an interest in sabotaging our water supply. A disaster of this scale would have to be something only our scientists could explain."

"Perhaps you are right, Mannion. We have been at this for weeks." With a disarmed and grateful demeanor, Rorke replied, "The truth is we have been hoping for answers that were easily explained in hopes of a simple fix. People are beginning to panic, and the signs posting contamination around the plant are driving public opinion and pressure. You know as well as I do that when we call on the scientists to get involved, concerns only increase."

Fear, despair, and anger were beginning to swell up within me, pouring into the size, depth, and width of my endless supply. The humans who depended on me were becoming suspicious and divided, desperate for a solution. Perhaps these scientists would be able to find a way to restore me.

The scientists spent many days taking samples from my supply and running many tests. One of them, whose name was Argon, decided to travel with a small team to take soil and core samples in the surrounding areas of the plant and the town bordering me. I remember the devastating conversation he had with Rorke and his team of researchers and developers.

"What are you saying to me, Argon?" said Rorke.

Argon was holding his journal and notes. He was stoic and appeared to be somewhat indifferent in his response. "We have extensively mapped the area and taken samples. Based on the topographic seismic documentation on record, relatively and comparatively, it appears there was a tectonic offset depositing excessive levels of geologically produced natural carcinogens into the arteries of the well."

"Please explain that in layman's terms, Argon." Said a somewhat frustrated Rorke.

"Amelia," Argon now deferring to his associate, "I think you could explain it better than me in layman's terms."

"There was a shift in the surrounding crust that caused naturally occurring harmful materials to be released into the water supply. Such occurrences, while most unfortunate, do occur and are usually unpredictable. The size of the shift would make it humanly impossible to correct, in our collective opinion." Amelia replied.

"Are you saying there is no hope for a fix to this?" Rorke said in an almost desperate tone.

Argon replied, "We would recommend that the well be abandoned and you begin to locate a new source of water in a location far from the current well."

My dismay only worsened with that proclamation. The feeling of abandonment and uselessness was more than I could bear. My despair and anger only led me to self-pity and sorrow. The researchers and developers discovered the problem, and the scientists understood what had happened to cause it, but no one could say why it happened, much less do anything to fix me.

"These things just happen," said the human scientist named Amelia, indifferently shrugging her shoulders.

"Such nonempathetic, incompetent humans," I thought to myself. How could they so easily turn their attention from me and dedicate all of it to the effort of finding another source of water? If those humans who established me could not fix me, and those who knew what had happened could not mend me, then it must be those who knew *why* this happened who would hold the solution to my problem. But what humans would they be? Where could they be found? I could only conclude that whoever they were, they must be cruel and twisted for being bystanders of this disaster in the first place.

Chapter 3 - Hope for Desperate Times

The town and the surrounding areas near me were suffering due to the lack of clean water. Gardens and farms were beginning to fail to produce food since they depended on a rigorous routine to draw from my reservoir and water the fields. My water was so toxic that the plants would suffer and die from the contamination. The rain was not enough to satisfy the requirement to maintain what was established by my existence. It took many years to bring my current state of efficiency to fruition. To make matters worse for the lost and hapless humans, their researchers and developers could not find any land close enough to establish a new source.

One of the townspeople named Felix decided to meet with the human referred to as "mayor." I have seen many of these mayors come and go since the town started. I have witnessed many of these humans do what they call "run for office." Often, they would solicit their worth through speeches from the gazebo, offering promises of making the town a better place. At the end of many days of these speeches and handshakes, all the humans would hold a contest by privately dropping slips of paper in a sealed box. The slips of paper with the name of their choice would be opened by trusted human officials and counted. Whoever had the most pieces of paper with their name on it became mayor, and they would be given power to decide on behalf of the town's interest. This mayor's name was Fredrick, and he agreed to meet with Felix at the beautiful gazebo just outside of the filtration plant.

I remember noticing in the past the two humans playing together in front of the gazebo. They were childhood friends attending the same school in town. I had heard them once say that they would never have met if it weren't the tradition of the school to sit all the students in alphabetical order by first name. They laughed about how students fought over seats until the teacher announced the rule. Felix and Fredrick always found themselves sitting next to each other, and from that they became friends. Their childhood friendship followed them to their adult years and continues to the present day.

The mayor, called Fredrick, had just arrived at the gazebo with another human who was acting as his personal scribe. The scribe's name was Ditimus. He carried with him a small, black, leather-bound record book in which he would take notes on behalf of the mayor. He was a weak-looking human who seemed to never be acknowledged by the others, as if he were a shadow following the mayor. And like it is with shadows, they tend to be ignored.

Felix was already at the gazebo, waiting patiently for the private meeting. Fredrick greeted Felix upon his arrival, "Well, hello, my good friend. So pleased to see you again. What good tidings do you bring me today?"

Felix responded nervously, "Hello, Fred." Then he turned to the scribe. "Hello, Ditimus." This was not the first time I noticed a human addressing another by a shorter version of their name. This, I have learned, is a way of affirming a personal friendship. Any other human would not have this privilege and would address the mayor as "sir" or "mayor" followed by the longer version of his name. "Thank you for taking the time to meet with me," said Felix to the mayor.

"Of course, of course, my dear friend," the mayor replied with a jovial tone while giving his friend a handshake. "And might I say, loyal supporter..." The last part was accompanied by an elbow nudge against Felix's side. "My interests are always in your direction when you call me," he concluded affectionately.

"Thank you, Fred," said Felix in response to the mayor's warm greeting. "I appreciate our friendship and the trust you place in me. I would like to talk to you about the crisis at hand."

The human mayor lowered his head, looking less jovial and more serious. He then looked up at Felix and replied, "Am I to expect more criticism and hostility over the events that have led to this town crisis?" Ditimus, quick to notice an opportunity, began to feverishly scribble in his journal, recording minutes of the impromptu meeting.

"No, Fred." Felix was once again calling the mayor by his personal name. "I know of a person who often visits our town. My son Darius and I believe he is very wise and could offer us insight and help on this matter. He is endowed with very old customs and methods that defy modern reason and science."

"Oh, you mean that ridiculous sage that wanders into our town for supplies and water from time to time?" replied the mayor. "If you ask me, he's very strange, and some believe he is mentally disturbed."

"Yes, Fred. I am aware of this, but these are desperate times, and quite frankly, we are out of options."

The mayor paused to think about Felix's proposal. "Can you arrange a meeting with him?" the mayor finally asked.

"I have already spoken to him about making arrangements to meet with the researchers, developers, scientists, and townspeople to hear him out...upon your approval, of course," answered Felix.

The mayor looked at Felix with a concerned and annoyed look. "I'm not certain going public without some vetting is such a good idea." Then he glanced over at his scribe, Ditimus, for a nonverbal opinion, as he had done many times before.

Ditimus, sensing the pause and noticing the mayor's eyes on him, stopped his note-taking and looked up. With a quick rattle of his head, he signaled "say no."

The mayor, now having Ditimus's mousey reply, paused again, looking down at the ground, as if to consider the advice. He then looked up with resolve, turning towards Felix. "You have my permission to confirm and facilitate the arrangements with the sage." Ditimus lowered his shoulders, his opinion on the matter once again rejected. "One more thing, Felix," added the mayor. "What is the sage's name?"

"His name is Pondurious."

The announcements were made throughout the town, and a couple of days afterwards, the townspeople were gathered, sitting in front of me, facing the gazebo. The town's maintenance and facility workers had set up the temporary seating that was common during such gatherings. They didn't seem to be the most comfortable seats. I noticed this while observing the spectators restlessly squirming. Also present were the scientist, Argon, and the researcher and developer, Rorke, both sitting next to each other on the right side of the gazebo, facing the crowd. Unlike the townspeople, they were enjoying protection from the sun by the canopy of the gazebo and had more comfortable seating. Despite that, they both looked annoyed and impatient. The others with prominent seating in the gazebo were the mayor, Fredrick, and his lifelong friend, Felix.

It was a bright, beautiful day with the sun shining and not a cloud in the crisp, steel-blue sky. The fall season had arrived, and there was enough of a chill in the air that they wore their jackets and had thin head coverings. A slight breeze was occasionally blowing while the large group of humans sat as comfortably as they could. There were nervous murmurs emanating from the gathering. Because of the circumstances and the fear for the future of their town, one could anticipate having undivided attention for the duration of what would turn out to be a long and intense gathering.

Mayor Fredrick stepped up to the podium area, and with a loud clearing of his throat, he barked out, "Citizens and good friends of this fine community!" The crowd noise diminished to complete silence, and all attention was directed at the mayor. Seeing he had the audience's undivided attention, he continued. "We all know the serious nature of what lies before us. Our once fresh and beautiful water supply has suffered a great catastrophe by being seriously contaminated. We have consulted our researchers and developers, along with our science department, and have found them to be without a solution to correct this tragic occurrence." The audience began to break out into a low, troubled murmur. Speaking over the noise, the mayor continued with more force in his voice. "We are here today to find hope and answers. A crisis like this requires positive attitudes and clear thinking. It also requires that we seek answers that may appear to defy logic." The audience was now beginning to show puzzled and concerned looks, and their voices were beginning to stir again. Noticing the change, the mayor quickly continued, "One of our fine citizens"—glancing over at Felix, who snapped to attention— "has made, in my opinion, a wise choice to solicit an authority who could provide us insight and direction to address this crisis." The crowd listened intently. "I would like to allow my dear associate, Felix, the opportunity to introduce our guest of honor."

The gathering of humans broke into mild applause, and Felix approached the front to address the crowd with obvious trepidation. The mayor warmly shook his hand and surrendered his spot at the podium to him. "Ahem, ahem." Felix nervously cleared his throat, paused, then finally spoke, "My fellow citizens, friends, and family. Many of us have at one time or another met the person I am about to introduce. We have welcomed him as one who has patronized our shops and enjoyed the benefits of our wonderful water supply. He is known for his words that mystify and cause us to ponder the principles and reasons behind life's meaning. He always seems to challenge us to consider these principles in situations, such as the one we find ourselves beholding. His words have offered us insights and answers that seem to defy our modern ways of looking at problems—suggestions that appear to challenge the very principles governed by science and our current sense of enlightenment." Now Felix had the crowd's attention. They simmered in anticipation of the introduction of the very human they were now being asked to hang their hopes on. Felix stood still, and with another nervous clearing of his throat, introduced the guest of honor, "Would you please welcome the sage, Pondurious." A brief tense pause of complete silence followed before the crowd erupted into a troubled rumble.

One of the humans in the crowd shouted out, "Are you serious, Felix? This man is a drifter and has offered counsel to my brother, which left him questioning his loyalty to our father's business!"

Another in the crowd mockingly barked, "You mean the man who comes to our town and has been telling others strange, mythical stories? He claims they are from another time!"

Followed by another human jumping in, shouting out, "I heard that he lives in a fantasy world!"

"Some question his sanity!" said another townsperson, while yet another barked out, "What good could listening to this man *really* do, Felix?!"

Then Felix found the strength in his voice to rise above the haranguing from the crowd. "People, people!" he shouted. When the contentious crowd quieted, hearing the desperate plea from Felix, he regained his composure. Calmly, he said, "The mayor of this town and I have decided on this course of action. I know I am not your voice of leadership, but you know that the mayor and I have been friends since childhood, and he trusts my opinion."

Breaking through the now quiet crowd was a new voice. It was coming from a young human sitting in the front row, close to the gazebo. He stood up and spoke directly to Felix. "Father," he said in a strong, youthful tone that all could hear. "You remember that Pondurious had spoken to us, warning sister of great trouble. Trouble that would come if we decided to welcome the stranger, Robert, into our family."

"Yes, I remember, Son," said Felix.

The young son of Felix, who was now facing his father while addressing the assembly, continued, "We all thought it very strange he would give such advice and risk being declared scandalous for not minding his own business. We also considered it gossip, which our family frowns upon. Mother, who has long since passed away and is missed dearly, was especially troubled by the advice he gave."

"Yes, son, this is true. We all found it odd that Pondurious had this foreknowledge. It was as if he could see the character of a man he had very little time to get to know."

"Yes, Father," said the young human called Darius. "We found that later, when Robert had moved onward to another town, a great trouble arose from him, and an innocent young woman was harmed. He was a person who was evil to other women, causing them much physical and mental harm. He had his sight set on sister, and we all were hopeful for the possibility of a happy union between the two. I believe Pondurious saved our family from a future tragic event." The crowd of humans erupted into a low murmur of conversation over Robert, who was proven to be scandalous.

Then Felix faced the crowd and spoke with conviction over the noise of the gathering, "Strangers and friends! I have seen no reason not to hear out the sage, Pondurious. He has proven to my family to be very helpful, wise, and good."

Then the mayor stood up, waving his hand in invitation for the sage to step forward. "And with that said, Pondurious, would you be so kind as to join us now?"

With those words, the mayor, the researcher and developer, the scientist, Felix, and his son faced the crowd, looking past them. The sage named Pondurious appeared from the rear and made his way slowly to the front, facing the great gazebo in front of me. There was a low murmuring from the crowd as he made his way up to the podium. He turned his head and smiled at young Darius, who was now positioned at the top step of the gazebo, seated against the handrail. He then turned his head slowly to face the crowd, preparing to speak. He was dressed as if he were a prospector or pioneer. His clothes were rugged and were made of animal skins to endure the elements. His cloak had a hood, which protected his head and gave him the look of a spiritual man. He had on his back a sack with shoulder straps. Above the sack was a bedroll that appeared to be made of exotic sheepskin. But what was most noticeable, and odd, was a clay amulet on a leather lace hanging around his neck. The amulet was somewhat crude, appearing to be very old. What stood out most about the amulet was the artistic impression of a very unusual symbol. The symbol looked like a royal seal one would see stamped in wax on correspondence from a time long ago.

When the townspeople had settled and all were silent, the sage addressed the crowd. "I want to thank you for the privilege of offering you a true story of old. This is so you may know of a hope which should never be lost. All things work for the good of all who understand and believe in the account I am about to share with you." The crowd was fixed in anticipation. He continued, "Before all that was known by us, and before all the universe existed, was the great and ever-present mystery W*hy*. This all-encompassing personality of truth and perpetual power was without the reliance of any other substance or thing. The personhood of the *Why* was and is always one with the personhood of the *Reason,* being fulfilled in the personhood of the *Mission*."

Pausing and seeing that he still had the attention of the silent crowd, Pondurious attempted to clarify what he was saying. "So, before the beginning of all the physical existence we comprehend, the personhood of the *Why* always existed. This was not a construct of human thought producing a question. The personhood of the *Why* has always been. And the *Why* has always been in relationship with the personhood of the *Reason*. And the personhood of the *Reason* has always been in fulfillment of the personhood of the *Mission*."

The researcher and developer, Rorke, rolled his eyes and commented under his breath, loud enough for Pondurious to hear, "Such a lofty, irrelevant statement. He's weaving a word-knot conundrum." Then, in front of everyone, he scorned the sage. "Obviously, Pondurious, you're a man who hasn't a clue how things are done in the real world. To say anything existed before all we know to be around us is madness."

The scientist, Argon, also took offense. "Pondurious," he snapped. "This is a most unscientific hypothesis. At least it is a broad and lofty paradox concluding a fool's dream of the physical." The scientist was indignant, attempting to reinforce his expertise in the sciences and them being superior to the sage's worldview.

The townspeople, who were provoked by the rude interruption, began to stir once more. They were puzzled by such words from the sage, straining to comprehend his abstract proclamation. "These concepts are mysterious and thought-provoking," one human in the crowd said to another.

"How can the meanings of the words *why, reason,* and *mission* be persons? This is a bizarre thing to say," said another human to the one next to him.

As I heard the swelling, perplexed conversations which had broken out from the human crowd, I began to doubt the mental integrity of the sage myself.

Pondurious then quelled the noise of the crowd by continuing with his voice raised, "Please, if I may!" He looked sternly at Rorke and Argon, then returned his attention to face the human gathering. "These three personalities, the *Why*, the *Reason*, and the *Mission,* exist in the perpetual, and the length, depth, and height of their realm is never-ending and with absolute, pure honesty. The *Why* is pure will, and the *Reason* is the complete revelation of the *Why*. Their perpetuality is seen fulfilled in the person of the *Mission,* proving all things possible." These even more mysterious and strange words had the effect of silencing the human crowd.

The sage took it as a sign to continue. "Even though they are three distinct entities, they are *one*. All they do by inspiration, purpose, and fruition can only exist as an invention of what is by their perpetual nature."

Then the young human called Darius asked the sage this question: "Sir, if all they do is by their perpetual nature, why do we not see any evidence of the perpetual in everything around us? In all things, we see there is a beginning and an end. It is self-evident that everyone born is destined to die."

Pondurious was for the moment silent, as if pleasantly taken aback by the power of observation and the conclusion of the young human. "You are seeing far ahead into the account I am sharing with you and your fellows. It is truly remarkable that you could consider that such a state of brokenness and decay could coincide with the absolute realm of perpetuality," answered the sage. "I find it very rare to see such ability to understand in one so apparently young as you. I extend to you a high compliment." The young human called Darius dared not question this proclamation from the sage. If anything, judging by his expression, he looked apprehensive and fearfully cautious from such a compliment.

Pondurious continued while the crowd remained still and focused on him. "Like an artist filled with a drive to express oneself, they created many works, including our universe, filled with the planets and all the things living on them. Their greatest accomplishment is humanity, which lives as if they created a self-portrait. Humanity was the dearest and most precious thing they made. They placed humanity at the highest place in their heart, honoring them as children of their own. They gave the humans dominion over all they made. All was meant to allow the way for humanity to desire and trust them. *They* being the *Why,* the *Reason,* and the *Mission.*"

Darius, who was having difficulty understanding what the sage was explaining, especially the idea of the three persons being one, asked him, "Does this united perpetual relationship of persons have *a* defining name to refer to their oneness?"

The sage's face then went pale, and the tone of his voice went from confident to what I would describe as reserved, reverent caution. What could possibly cause such noticeable fear and pause, giving a name to the very nature of the *Why*, *Reason,* and the *Mission?* After all, he did say they were one, so I would think one name would be a reasonable thing to ask of the sage. But after an awkward pause, Pondurious exhaled a long sigh and said, "It is impossible to find a name best describing the character and nature of the paradox of this relationship. It is not in our ability to fully comprehend these *Three* persons in a relationship. Such a never-ending, all-present, united existence of personhoods cannot host a name, or to put it simply, be contained in the perimeter of our minds." Noticing the tense anticipation of the crowd, Pondurious continued, "Perhaps it would help our understanding to call this omnipresent relationship by the three natures of who they are. So let us use *W* for the *Why,* who is pure will; *R* for the *Reason*, who being the perfect revelation of the *Why*; and *M* for the *Mission,* who is the absolute fulfillment of the *Why* and the *Reason*. These initials of each form the acronym *WRM*." Pondurious paused. Darius and some in the assembly were slowly nodding their heads as if they were following his logic, so the sage continued, "The personhood of the *Why,* which is the initial *W,* will not be shown because He cannot be seen in the physical. This is because the personhood of the *Why* is pure will, anonymous to our minds. So, we are left with only being able to comprehend, as it is revealed to us, the persons of the *Reason* and the *Mission*. This acronym spells RAM, which is the *Reason and Mission,* while the *Why* is not seen or spoken. So, for the sake of simplicity, and with no less reverence and respect, let us call the relationship of the three persons *Ram*. And since these persons have always been, and will always be, in a relationship as one, we will also refer to them as *Ram the perpetual*." When he looked around at the crowd, Pondurious saw some apprehensively nodding in acceptance, while others, which included the scientist and developer, began murmuring among themselves.

"Not sure this hodgepodge of rules you've constructed holds any water, no pun intended," one person in the crowd blurted out in a snarky tone. Some began to laugh.

"I thought you were a sage, not a whacked-out wordsmith," jeered another.

But others in the assembly were more reserved, having puzzled and troubled looks on their faces.

Raising her hand and her voice, trying to be heard above the others, another human expressed her concerns. "This is all *most* abstract and troubling, Pondurious. You've only managed to conjure some elaborate conundrum, or something circular like that!"

"Yes, Pondurious, what kind of dog-chasing-his-tail nonsense is this?" blurted out another human.

"How can you make a person out of such things as a question, answer, and purpose?" barked out another. The intensity of the noise of the crowd began to grow again, with rapid-fire interrogational eruptions being hurled randomly from the townspeople.

Pondurious had a calm and reserved countenance on his face, as if not surprised by their reaction, while the crowd continued increasing in the boil. He quelled the crescendo by calmly shouting over the rabble, "Good people, good people!" The crowd noise simmered down. Seeing that the audience had been brought back into focus, Pondurious continued, "Dear friends, please try to believe me that I am only setting the stage for a series of world-changing events I am about to share with you. As best as you can understand the meaning of what I am trying to describe, try to bring it forward with you by allowing your minds to remain open. It will prove to be valuable in understanding what I am attempting to share with you. It is my conviction that this is what is necessary to fulfill the very purpose for which I was summoned before you. You will need to trust that what I have said is important for you to understand. It is my hope that all will comprehend, and it will reveal the answers you are looking for. So please, return to me your attention, and be patient, for the sake of all gathered here today."

Darius's young voice rang out in the silence that followed. "I believe and trust you, Pondurious. Yes, it is all mysterious and strange, but a voice inside of me compels me to trust you."

Pondurious smiled at the young human, son of the human called Felix, then said, "Thank you, young man."

Chapter 4 - The Great Plot Against Ram the Perpetual

After a difficult attempt to define the mysterious personhood of Ram, the human sage called Pondurious continued, "Try to comprehend that all reality we experience exists in the immense expanse of the grand and glorious construct of Ram the perpetual. Our very consciousness is present in it and part of this construct." At this statement, many in the crowd began to show strained expressions of bewildered lack of understanding. Pondurious paused, glanced around, then attempted to drill down into this thought to clarify. "It is a glorious work, our universe and all contained in it. It majestically demonstrates the very nature and power of Ram. All being created by Him to fulfill His expression of His nature and purposeful design."

Pondurious was describing the vast universe, which the human scientists all held in the highest regard. This was their area of expertise. The knowing of the nature of everything while trying to understand the idea of the nothingness of space was a never-ending debate among themselves. The human scientist named Argon spoke up to challenge Pondurious. "Pondurious, I think I speak for most of our leaders in science about the complexity and expanse of our universe. But few in our field, if any, would believe it is contained in the realm of anything like this mythical perpetual existence you call *Ram*."

Pondurious questioned Argon, "So, if you are claiming Ram is a myth, then are you saying He doesn't really exist, Argon? Wouldn't that be a scientific impossibility to prove something *doesn't* exist?"

Argon shook his head as if he sneeringly disapproved of the question. However, he had no rebuttal.

The sage continued by speaking of the laws and principles governing Ram's construct, such as physics and ethics. "These and many, many others prove the very nature of Ram, which is unmovable and sustained by Him. Ram is the absolute truth. Ram, being the absolute truth, is just, having dominion over the extent of His created universe. He is the author of all laws which govern the physical and the ethical."

The researcher and developer named Rorke had a more interesting and engaging response and question to what Pondurious was claiming. "I would agree with you,

Pondurious, that there are immovable laws and principles that guide decision-making and how things work. My service to this town depends on them. But I am having trouble believing that the physical I work in is more than a natural cause and effect alone. I do not see any physical evidence that would prove this so-called 'personhood' is behind these laws, which would prove your case. Even if this personhood existed, how could you ever have any provable knowledge of it? Or to put it this way, how can a fish inside its bowl ever be able to look outside of it by its own ability?"

Pondurious answered Rorke with, "Or how can a blind man experience sight if he has never seen?"

Rorke then nodded. "Yes, Pondurious, your question says it even better." Rorke, appearing to see eye to eye with the sage, was now certain he had Pondurious backed in a corner.

Pondurious then answered, saying, "It would require the man with sight to describe *sight* to the blind man. The blind man would need to have unwavering trust in the man with sight. But even then, he would not have experienced seeing, even though the existence of the ability to see is still a fact. The blind man's experience of sight can only exist by completely trusting and believing the one who has sight."

Rorke seemed annoyed by Pondurious's answer and, like Argon, had nothing more to say. The young man named Darius interrupted the silence, addressing Pondurious. "Sir, we have been given no reason not to believe you. Please continue your dissertation so that we might trust and believe in how it may help us in this crisis."

I was now beginning to shed my doubt in this human sage and was also anxious for him to continue.

The sage smiled again at the young man and continued, "Among the many other wonderful things Ram the perpetual had fashioned were the stewards. These stewards were endowed with great power and beauty to serve Ram faithfully and wonderfully. But there was one of them who was exceptionally powerful and beautiful, who, in his vanity and pride, became resentful and angry that Ram would use him for service. This indignant steward, with a swelling resentment for Ram, decided he was superior to the other stewards. *'Certainly, special exceptions should be made for my own sake,'* he reasoned. *'At the very least, I should rule the lesser stewards,'* he grumbled. As time went on, the vain and beautiful steward of Ram grew to be more boastful and contemptuous towards the other stewards, and even more so towards Ram, who made him. His resentment grew to rage, even to the point of wanting to destroy everything Ram had made. He was hopelessly blinded by his swollen pride and hatred. He was driven by an obsession to overrule Ram, who was the source of all things. He had crossed the line and reached the point of no return. His heart had become forever sealed in a lost state of sadistic ambition."

The thought that anyone could become so bent and irredeemably twisted stunned the crowd into silence.

Pondurious continued, "One day, the rebellious steward had a fantastic idea. If he could convince other stewards that they, too, were being denied everything due to them, then perhaps he could form an army big enough to overthrow or destroy Ram. He would rule over everything, making him greater than Ram Himself. His first step in this treasonous plan was to convince as many of Ram's stewards of its merit. There were many that were persuaded to join him in this cosmic overthrow of the dominion of Ram the perpetual. But Ram knew of what was being planned and knew this would happen, even before the conception of the steward's sinister plot. Ram declared the rebellious steward beyond restitution and was banished along with his legions of followers. Ram was right in doing this since the rebellious steward and his followers had committed an unforgivable act of high treason. Why Ram showed mercy on the treasonous legions and their forsaken steward who led them is a mystery to be revealed later."

Darius questioned Pondurious again, "Sir, if Ram knew ahead of time that they would commit treason, why did he create them in the first place?"

The sage answered Darius, "This is a great question, young man. One which is key to understanding all the content of my message. But the answer can only come if you listen and understand the whole account. As I have tried to explain, it will reveal itself later."

"Yes, of course, sir," Darius replied. "Forgive my impatience."

"I would not call it impatience, young man, but timing *is* everything." Then the sage continued, "The treasonous steward, along with his followers, was no longer permitted to be in the presence of Ram. They were banished to exist in Ram's *grand and glorious design,* separated and outside of his presence, except for appealing a grievance or case. Because of this separation, they were destined to never know anything good. All that is wicked, hateful, deceitful, and malicious would be the only purpose they would ever know. This was not because Ram was cruel to them, but this was the natural result of their choice to mutiny against Ram's perpetual infinite greatness. There could never be any hope for a restoration. Because of their resolve and the unforgivable consequence of their treason, the darkness in them only grew. The cast-out stewards began to make plans for their retribution of Ram. If they could find a way to harm Ram to the point that He would surrender, then the possibility of the mutinous stewards stealing Ram's dominion was within reach. They salivated at the possibility that their existence could go beyond the perpetual!"

"This is quite the story." Pondurious was once again interrupted by Argon. "Are we to believe this is *not* a fiction? The idea of creatures that are made by someone not knowing the potential for treason questions the integrity of your so-called *Ram*. It would be like a scientist allowing a mixture of potassium and water in a container not worthy to withstand the explosive reaction. If this *Ram the perpetual* is great enough to author all the mysteries of our existence, surely, he would foresee this."

Rorke added, "This is where the science and I agree. When we propose a plan to build, we would never lay a foundation on ground that is shifting and contains properties that would fail to host a worthy foundation. To anyone who thinks logically, it would be pure insanity to attempt to do such a thing. These fictional stewards would have to be mad if they really believed this."

Then the mayor, Fredrick, rose up from his seat. "Gentlemen gentlemen," he said in a calm and somewhat patronizing tone. "I understand the idea of the contradiction you are seeing. But being the politician that I am, I have to say, when it comes to ego and ambition, I would be the first to tell you one can be led to do rash and illogical things."

The gathering broke out into laughter while the mayor smiled as if he had won the argument over the esteemed representatives of the town.

Then a towns-person jokingly barked out over the laughter, "Spoken like the true fallen steward that you are, Mayor!" The crowd's laughter became a roar while the mayor's countenance went from pleased with himself to annoyed scorn, and he abruptly sat down.

The mayor's close friend, Felix, nervously stood up and spoke loudly over the roar of laughter, "All right, all right! People, please!" The noise began to simmer down. "Yes, we all get the joke, and I know the mayor takes it all in good fun, but let us please allow our honored guest to continue. Please, Pondurious, we meant no disrespect."

The sage did not seem to mind the interruption. He seemed to be enjoying the playful exchange of egos, watching it with a satisfied demeanor. With a pleasant, soft smile on his face, he continued the story, "But believe they did, and sought obsessively to destroy and injure all Ram had commissioned. They sought to influence and persuade all the invention of Ram with the sinister hope of causing the universe and all which exists in Ram's beautiful expression to lose all perpetuality."

Then Darius interrupted, "How could they possibly accomplish this?"

The sage answered, "I will elaborate later, but for now, please believe me that humanity was to be the linchpin to the fallen steward's plan. Because of the innocence of humanity, Ram's most precious work, the fallen steward and his followers, could only influence with their delusional and manipulative words of propaganda. Ram would never allow torture or those types of coercive methods to force humanity to rebel against Him. But free speech reflects the nature of Ram and conforms to the construct that humanity was made to be free-thinking entities. Nothing else could support self-will coming to desire and trust in Ram. So, this freedom was given as Ram's loving way to allow humanity to come willingly to Him. No other of his great works had been given such a loving gift. And it was because of this special gift that the fallen steward truly believed he could succeed."

Pondurious paused at this point, seeing that the crowd around him was mesmerized and silent, like children hanging onto every word. Whether they comprehended what he was saying or were more like an audience watching an elaborate magic trick unfold before them, he continued explaining. The sage's voice took on a quieter and more serious tone. "So, this means of all that Ram the perpetual spoke into existence, what was most precious to Him was humanity. Humanity was placed in a position even higher than the most beautiful steward, and all his legions now waging bloody war against Ram's dominion. This was what the fallen steward despised most of all in Ram's perpetual invention. He had to be thinking to himself, *'How dare he place such weak creatures above my authority!'*"

Then the sage paused briefly. I saw sadness in his expression. Perhaps he was reflecting on how weak and helpless humanity really is. Or perhaps it was sadness for the fallen steward, who was once a beautiful and significant creature, becoming so hopelessly lost.

"Sir?" Darius called out, seeing the troubled look on the sage's face. "You seemed to imply earlier that Ram's desire is that we desire and trust Him. Is it possible to break the heart of Ram if we refuse to do so? Isn't this what the fallen steward is saying that he believes?"

Pondurious snapped out of his sad, reflective pause to answer. "It is important to distinguish between the will and the desire of Ram, young man. His will for us is that we seek to fulfill it in our free will. His desire for us is His expression of his never-ending love for us. They are *not* the same thing."

The young man looked down in silence. His countenance became pensive after this answer. Slowly raising his head to make eye contact with the sage, he responded, "I think I now understand why you appeared to be sad, sir."

The sage gave the young man a slow, appreciative smile. I am not certain why he did this. I sensed that there was a hidden understanding that they both had established in their hearts and minds. Pondurious did not elaborate on this and continued, "Here I need to explain that Ram's perpetual work is not the same as His perpetual realm. Ram's perpetual realm is always with no beginning and no end. However, Ram's perpetual work began when it was fashioned by Him. It could only remain perpetual if it remained joined and sustained by Ram. All the stewards who are meant to serve Ram in his perpetual realm do not reside in this constructed perpetual work. This work is known to us as the universe, planets, and all living on them. One might describe this perpetual work as a glorious and beautiful museum full of magnificent and wondrous creations of art. Each piece, in its own way, is a unique and precious expression of the very nature of Ram. Both Ram and his loyal stewards frequent this marvelous museum, but their home is the perpetual realm existing always. For Ram, every visit was a celebration and offered him great satisfaction. But for the apostate stewards, it was a vile and ugly place they were now forced to live in. They had been exiled into the perpetual work of Ram to stumble and lurk about until the final sentence for their treachery could be fulfilled. They are filthy, lost, wicked, deceitful, and desperate homeless fugitives."

The sage paused again to see if all around him were still with him. Some had expressions on their faces like small children being read a wonderful bedtime story. Others appeared to have stern looks with folded arms, as if they were beginning to lose patience. Some had sneering expressions as if they were wondering why they had wasted time hearing any of this. I had no choice but to listen to the end since I didn't have any feet to leave with, and my situation was desperate and hopeless.

Pondurious continued, "Ram's most favorite place in the great museum was with the humans he had sculpted with great love and care. Everything he had made prior to them reflected his own creative imagination. But the humans were different in that they were self-portraits of the very nature and character of Ram Himself. Such was the beauty, complexity, and character of humanity. So, Ram cherished them as if they were His dearest children. Ram poured so much of His likeness into this one piece; humanity occupied the most accessible and closest room, just at the foothills of Ram's perpetual realm. Like a loving father, Ram longed for them to desire him as such. They were like trees planted to bear the fruit of trust and love for Him who was responsible for their very existence."

I thought to myself, *how could they not love Ram? Look what Ram gave them! All the mystery and beauty of a wonderful planet filled with every pleasure and abundance to meet all their needs!* What the human sage called Pondurious said next troubled me beyond the depth and width of my liquid reach.

"Ram allowed himself to be vulnerable to humanity," the sage announced. "Ram allowed that all it would take to ruin His perpetual work was to reject Him and adopt the spirit of rebellion and ungratefulness. Ram had to allow this, for it would never be possible for humanity to desire and trust Him if they were made to do it." Pondurious paused and continued in a loud and dramatic tone, which startled the crowd. "'*This is the very thing which will make all my hideous desires come true,*' proclaimed the leader of the insubordinate legion of stewards! Like a fierce, deranged, and tyrannical dictator addressing his unruly subjects, it came to him. The most sinister, delightful, and wicked idea. If this great fallen steward could convince humanity to never desire and trust Ram, then all the perpetual work Ram had done would join in the exile from top to bottom. The malicious steward was confident this physical perpetual existence would crumble from the very highest reach by the very likeness of Ram joining his legions in this sinister mission. All Ram found delight in would be taken away, which would surely give the lord steward power over Ram. Vile and sickening ecstasy, the lord steward was now beginning to feel. For the first time, he began to salivate disgusting-looking, thick drool at the thought. '*Such debilitating and devastating heartbreak Ram would experience,*' the despot steward must have been thinking to himself. Then the twisted, smiling, and drooling steward embodied a creature of the perpetual work of Ram and crept menacingly towards one of the humans. He must have been filled with delight that his plan was now beginning to develop nicely."

Chapter 5 - Man and the Treacherous Steward Meet

The human assembly was now thick into what the sage named Pondurious was explaining, so he continued, "In the time that all of Ram's created work thrived, and flourished, man also was part of this perpetual existence. All men, women, and children did not know of any suffering or death. This perpetual state of existence withheld strife or conflict since all needs were met, and perfect harmony abounded. The knowledge of Ram was very present in all the beauty, order, and balance a perpetual existence would promote. The voice of Ram was heard as if an inner voice in each person spoke when questions were asked or Ram chose to speak to them. It was as if the minds of humanity were joined with the mind of Ram. Ram did not allow the connection to be a violation of the beauty and individuality of everyone. A sovereign existence which allowed Ram to remain respectfully anonymous was what Ram desired. Like a father and his children, He would be ever ready to be there to help and answer any questions they may have. This was so his beloved humanity could fully enjoy and find Ram among His created work."

The young human named Darius spoke up, interrupting Pondurious. "How wonderful a thought, but surely this is not what we see today. What happened, sir?" he asked the sage.

Pondurious paused and gave Darius a kind smile. Then he continued, "One day, a man named Alphamis was enjoying the sweet smell of honeysuckle in the air while resting. He was sitting with his back against a stout and very old quince tree in a forest filled with shade and other delicious fruit trees. He could hear the soothing sound of a waterfall in the near distance while the fields were filled with beautiful, colored birds singing harmonious songs. He sat serenely with his eyes closed and head leaning back against the tree while his hand was running his fingers through the lush green mossy bed under him. He, like all others, was at peace, and life was one serene day after another. He was always happy to be in Ram's presence and looked forward to times when he would sit and talk with Him."

Darius and all the others in the crowd seemed to be enjoying this account of the past. It was a very pleasant scenario that the sage was sharing with the crowd. Even the humans who were more confrontational, such as Argon and Rorke, were also captivated by this beautiful thought of such an existence. I, being very old and knowing many, many generations of humans, could not recall any such time the sage was speaking of. Surely it must have been very long ago. Long before my first encounter with the humans and the deer. Perhaps even before my existence came to be.

The sage continued. "Alphamis, while reclining, suddenly was interrupted from his restful, pensive thoughts, and his eyes were opened by a stirring noise in front of him. The startling sight of the fallen steward appeared in Ram's forest as some kind of crawling, slime-coated, oversized four-legged creature, which made its way to where Alphamis reclined. Because the fallen steward had to take a form which could be experienced in the man's realm, it could not be human. Alphamis was startled, not recognizing this creature who was slimy, dark, and unusual in size. It appeared to resemble the other animals on the planet, requiring external heat to keep them warm. Some of the animals, including all men such as himself, did not require external heat but generated heat from within themselves. Such was not the case with this freakish-looking creature."

"It sounds like you are describing a rather large salamander, Pondurious," interjected the scientist, Argon.

"Not exactly, Argon." Pondurious continued, "It was able to speak to the man. His speech was like a swishing, chilling wind, which would invoke emotions and thoughts in the man." Pondurious paused and then continued, "The menacing, slimy steward began to speak, but not in words like all men and women had among themselves, but as Ram himself would speak to them. *'Loved of Ram,'* said the fallen steward. With a liquid-dark and alluring voice, he continued, *'You are most beautiful and intelligent. You are above all that Ram has created. You are even held in higher regard than I am and all I rule.'*"

Then the young Darius interrupted Pondurious with an inspired question, "If the fallen steward came to Alphamis to turn his heart away from Ram, why did he speak the truth to him? You just described how Ram viewed man as his most precious expression of his creation. Wouldn't speaking the truth only solidify the man's resolve to remain loyal to Ram?"

The sage answered Darius in a complimentary tone. "Young man," he said, before pausing with a kind and endearing smile. "You are most bright and observant. You are at the precipice of understanding one of the greatest truths one can hope to know. Keep that thought in front of you, as it will serve to help you understand what happens next."

Darius nodded with a convinced assurance. "Yes, of course, sir."

Then Pondurious continued to tell the story. "Alphamis began to experience in his heart a feeling he had never really felt before. For the first time, he considered himself of great worth and of special privilege. Until this point in time, he had only experienced joy and peace that comes from knowing Ram. He had never had any need to question Ram's motives. But there was a side to all humanity that had yet to be revealed."

The young Darius was quick to ask Pondurious, "What could possibly not have been revealed, sir?"

"Ego, young man. Man was like an innocent child with every need being met. He had no reason to consider himself against any other human, but especially not against Ram. All needs were met, and self-preservation was not on his mind because of the perpetual existence he enjoyed."

"I think I understand, sir. It makes perfect sense to me," replied Darius.

Pondurious continued, "Then the man called Alphamis asked the fallen steward this question: '*Who and what are you, and why are you speaking to me?*' The fallen steward answered the man, '*My name cannot be spoken in this perpetual place that you exist in, but like you, I am very great and powerful in Ram's dominion.*'"

"Why could his name not be spoken, sir?" Darius asked the sage.

Pondurious explained, "The fallen steward's name could not be heard or spoken by man because of man's innocence." Darius nodded, as if this satisfied his question, so Pondurious continued, "Then Alphamis said to the fallen steward, '*You are describing who you are and not saying your name. You have also told me who you are by comparing me to you. But you have not said why you are here, telling me these things.*'"

The sage then continued with how the fallen steward answered Alphamis, "'*I have come to inform you that Ram has been keeping a secret from you. He knows that if you ever realize how great and powerful you really are, then you would never have need for Him, and he would lose your loyalty. Although he is mighty beyond all that is known, he knows if you ever found out your true nature, you would see that you are just a captured thing that he could eventually grow tired of and discard into the cosmic heap of his realm.*'"

Then Pondurious shared with the crowd a most puzzling statement from the man called Alphamis.

"This creature has revealed something that until now has eluded me. I take for granted all the times I have been able to just reach forward, and all things were before me. I have never needed anything. Could it be that Ram is some sort of maligned herdsman, and I am captive to His whims? How do I know that Ram is nothing more than anything else that exists before me? Is He hiding that He is subject to me? Is it possible He relates to me only for the sake of good standing? Is He being honest with me?"

With the advent of Alphamis's questions, Pondurious revealed to his audience an incredible shift in the circumstances. "The questions swirled in Alphamis's head," said the sage. "Something new began to grow in Alphamis's heart. He began to doubt the goodness of Ram, and resentment began to grow inside of him. It was like a burning fire in a very dry brush that started small but very quickly began to reach the point where it was out of control. The sensation overwhelmed Alphamis, and he began to fear and resent the idea of his next conversation with Ram. Usually, he would meet Ram in one of the areas in the beautiful meadow, but he decided not to show up on this occasion. The meeting place was for the sake of Alphamis, so when he determined to not be there, Ram revealed Himself to Alphamis where he was."

This troubled the young Darius. "How could Alphamis believe that he could hide from Ram? Understanding what you explained about Ram's nature, is there really any place you *could* hide? Is Ram able to hide anything He has done from Himself?

The sage answered Darius, "Young man, I said that Ram revealed Himself to the man. You are correct to conclude that Alphamis could not hide from Ram even though Ram had allowed anonymity. But this was the beginning of all being undone. The first evidence of this truth was that Alphamis thought he could hide from Ram. But the sad reality of this truth is that Ram was now hidden from Alphamis."

The young man responded, "Well, yes, I think I see what you are explaining, sir." Then, after a brief pause, Darius spoke up once again. "I find it very intriguing that no one hides from Ram. If he is the author of all we experience, then it is logical that he misses nothing and is aware of everything."

"I am very impressed with the way your mind works, young man," complimented the sage. "Once again, you have come to a profound and wise conclusion."

Then, with an empathetic tone of concern, the young Darius asked the sage, "What is Ram going to do with the man? Will Ram punish him for believing what the fallen steward said?" The crowd began to snap out of their intrigue with the questions and the banter between the young man and the sage. The questions from Darius broke their focus. The assembly of humans began to erupt into murmuring among themselves.

The mayor rose from his seat to address the crowd. "Please, everyone, allow Pondurious to continue. If everyone would please remain quiet so we all can hear." Then the noise from the crowd settled down for the sage to continue.

Pondurious shared the next part, which greatly troubled Darius. "Alphamis, now in the presence of Ram with his head held high in defiance, questioned Him in a cold voice, *'Why have you lied to me, Ram? How could I ever trust you again?'* Then the treacherous steward began to laugh and was full of wicked delight, knowing he had set into motion the destruction of all of Ram's perpetual work. A new thing began to appear and develop in the mighty picture Ram had painted. Although nothing existing in Ram's Museum is new, since all things come from Ram, like a dormant cancer introduced for the first time, the law of entropy was unleashed into all that Ram had made. All for Ram's purpose, lying in wait, this law was to be the fall of everything."

Then Darius's father, Felix, spoke up. "Pondurious, I think my son and I are both finding this most interesting but also disturbing. Are we really to believe that man is the center of Ram's created universe and what decisions we make directly affect everything?"

The scientist jumped in, "I am very familiar with the law of entropy. Why would your so-called 'author of everything' ever allow such a law to exist if He were perpetual? Perhaps the man Alphamis in your story is correct that this person you call *Ram* is just some other creature or being like the fallen steward you describe."

The sage replied, "Nothing in Ram's dominion is unexpected or unplanned. All His works are in unity to fulfill His will and desires. All He is and does is forever good."

Then Rorke interjected his thoughts, "I see nothing good here, Pondurious. The man you say was called Alphamis is an ungrateful, unforgiving jackass. He sees himself as the center of the universe and the owner of it. Where is this *forever good* in these things you are telling us?"

The mayor stood up and addressed Rorke, "Please, Rorke, we invited Pondurious here to help with the crisis at hand. I don't believe he is trying to mislead or contradict the facts of his account. Let's continue to be patient and let him finish explaining."

"It's quite all right, Mayor Fredrick," said Pondurious. "The account I am presenting builds on many principles, and your friends here are not unlike many others I have tried to explain them to." The sage turned once more to face the gathering, picking up where he left off, "So, *Reason* and the *Mission* became cut off from the human race. The man severed his relationship with Ram. The existence of the universe, planets, and all living on them ceased to be sustained by the perpetual. All of Ram's created work was now ruled and governed by the law of entropy, which is His law. This meant that instead of the universe forever expanding and becoming more and more, it began to accelerate towards atrophy and dissipation. Stars, which were meant to live forever, began to collapse, bringing all matter and light towards themselves. The planets began to cool instead of remaining steady and established. The crust of the planet we live on began to crack and shift, making the surface less and less compatible to sustain the beautiful works of Ram. All Ram had lovingly built was now dying. Every creature reacted to the circumstances, which were a harsh and traumatic reality. Some creatures could no longer find food that had existed during the perpetual connected state and were driven to find new and hostile substitutes. The oceans became a precarious place for all sea life, where the order of tranquility was destroyed by this new dynamic. The lands began to divide and rupture with cracks, releasing the dying lifeblood of the core, which once lived and sustained all life but was now decaying. But what was worst of all was that humanity no longer acknowledged the goodness of Ram but became reliant on themselves. Each was led by their own desires and ambitions. They became petty and would struggle to become greater than the other. They were blinded to the wisdom of Ram and sought their own wisdom inside themselves. Dividing and conquering became the new and only way. This was the very result the wicked steward had hoped for. He began shrieking thunderous laughter and beat his chest at the sick thrill of what he had done. All Ram had so cherished was now undone, including the most precious and dearest to Him...humanity."

Argon spoke to the sage from his position in the front, "Well, Pondurious, I can't argue with your logic. If you set a stage, any possible scenario can be performed on it, whether it is based on truth or falsehood. You can even mix truth with falsehood and make the plot work. Certainly, science can't argue with the law of entropy and how it plays a part in what we call *good science*. But I am not able to accept this truth mixed with fiction idea, a concept dictating its beginning. The idea of the *perpetual* is in theory only. No one has ever been able to prove it is a reality. I long for the *sacred* discovery of something perpetual and consider the possibility intensely. As a scientist, I can see the phenomenon of energy leaving one system of matter and moving onward to disperse into alternate matter. I can agree the original source of all energy had a beginning, but I cannot accept your so-called *perpetual relationship* starting it. Even more unacceptable is the intention to maintain it indefinitely through being connected to itself. No one in science has ever been able to make a self-sustaining power source maintaining a system indefinitely."

Argon clearly could not accept this order of things Pondurious was trying to explain. It seems to me that Argon's pride and intellect determined that the perpetual should come from the existing known laws and could only happen from the invention of an evolving intellect. It was as if Argon was confident this was something science would one day stumble into and would be very happy to take credit for it. To Argon, Pondurious was just mixing truth with lies to justify his story.

Pondurious replied to Argon's narrative, "Trying to be respectful of your knowledge, Argon, you are making my point and have shown that you understand what I am explaining much more than you realize. It is this whole idea that truth can be mixed with untruth. It would be far better that we have never known truth than to live as both are one in the same." This once again left the scientist with nothing more to say.

Darius chimed in, "Could you shed some light on why, in this case, it would be better to never know the truth, sir? I cannot picture our world without truth. We would be aimlessly rebounding into everything. The quality of our lives would suffer greatly. Despair and hopelessness would abound everywhere."

Pondurious answered the young Darius, "Yes, of course you are correct, young man. I am sharing all of this to allow you to see how important this one idea of truth really is. Earlier, I had said that you are at the precipice of understanding one of the greatest truths one can hope to know. This being that one would be able to know the truth and be able to know it from the lie. To not know the truth from the lie is to exist as you do now. It is to exist in a state of enslaved living death." After saying this, all that could be heard was the whispering sound of the cool autumn breeze blowing through the rafters of the gazebo and the faint sounds of the surrounding trees dropping their remaining dead leaves.

Then it suddenly dawned on me. Mankind was just like me, a well fixed in one immovable spot and at the mercy of a broken, dying existence. I began to ponder how Ram's intention could possibly be this way. This planet I depended on was in a spiraling downward state of decay. The entire universe was accelerating towards cosmic death. The humans who depend on me, although responsible for this broken universe, were lured into it by a very clever and insidious bait and switch. This fallen steward was the most deplorable and lost thing Ram had devised. How could the one who has the power to do *anything* permit this? I still hear my paraphrased words of the scientist echoing, "Wouldn't foreknowledge of a backstabbing steward, bent towards anarchy, not escape Ram's sight?" The sage did say this answer was a mystery to be revealed later. This did nothing to comfort me. My reality proved only what had happened and the state I am now in. My despair and depression were now making me wish I were a developer who had the heavy machines needed to demolish my existence to the sum of dirt. As if it couldn't get any worse, I had no means before me to end my own existence.

Then the young Darius broke the silence once again by asking the sage, "Sir, if Ram so loved His work, especially humanity, why would He ever tolerate all of it dying?" At these words, the crowd began to stir with a low rumble of questioning tones. "How could this possibly serve Ram?" Darius added. Then, with a tone of the deepest concern in his voice, and as the crowd noise continued to swell, the young man concluded by asking, "What about this mystery to be revealed you spoke of earlier, and does it hold the answer?" His final question was met by a content and confident response from Pondurious.

Chapter 6 - Reason and Mission of the Why

The young man Darius had just asked Pondurious a series of questions, which also caused the crowd to stir. It was clear Darius was troubled, so the sage assured the young man to put his mind to rest. "My dear curious and troubled friend!" Pondurious said, cutting over the crowd noise. For the first time, the sage addressed Darius as "friend." I was beginning to see that there was something the sage saw in the young man that began to give him reason to call Darius such. As the crowd noise began to settle down, the sage turned outward to face them. "All that is being explained to you is so you might know good tidings of life-changing news. It is my hope that if you know, then you will come to understand Ram the perpetual has done a most wonderful thing beyond your imagination."

The gathered assembly of humans was again silent and focused on Pondurious. Seeing the crowd was now fixed on him, he continued, "I am one of a following who live life by a wonderful revelation of truth, hope, and excellence. The witness of this historic landmark has been passed down through many generations, starting with the firsthand account of a small group of people. They were close friends with a man who possessed exceptional qualities beyond any other person they had ever known. Most people this man encountered found they could relate to him. He had an uncommon humility, which made him approachable, disarming, and likable. To be more concise, when he spoke and acted, he did so with meekness, giving him a persuasive power to change hearts and minds. But what made him stand out most of all was a noticeable serenity in his countenance and a genuine, affectionate appreciation of others."

Then the young man's father, Felix, interrupted the sage. "This man you are referring to, Pondurious... who was he and where was he from?"

The sage answered, "Not who he *was,* Felix, but who he *is,* as I will soon explain. He is from an area that is still considered ordinary and not especially renowned in its reputation. Today it is called by a different name, but at the time it was known as the Primus Regions."

The mayor stood up suddenly and interrupted Pondurious, "Well, that is certainly something! I have always been interested in the explorations and discoveries of strange ancient lands. There is a publication I enjoy very much which writes about such places and cultures. Being a mayor, I find it helpful to study such subjects so I can better serve my own town. Understanding different areas and the people who live there helps me in my governing. It is an amazing coincidence that a couple of months ago I was reading about that area called the Primus Regions. It is many miles from here, across our great eastern ocean, and the modern people living there today hold a legendary claim to an old story of their past involving a young innocent woman. Her story was about finding herself pregnant but claiming to have never had a relationship with a man. Of course, it was quite a scandal when the child was born. He grew up with the stigma of the scandal, but it was said his mother rejected any ridicule over it. She found help in a good man who married her, and they raised the child as their own. As the child grew up, he became wise and demonstrated great leadership capabilities. It was said as an adult, he was well-known and did many amazing things."

"Yes, Mayor Fredrick," the sage replied. "I am quite impressed that you know about this man and his time."

The mayor, seeming pleased with himself, drew a wide, pleasant smile and glanced around with a satisfied expression on his face. Then he slowly sank back to his seat. His mousey scribe Ditimus, who was sitting in the crowd in front, began to scribble frantically in his book. He was recording the mayor's every move so that much could be said about his leadership in the town's news publications. Having shown a working proficient knowledge of such things was unusual for the mayor, so it was newsworthy for the scribe to record the interruption.

"But there is still much more to be known about this man," added Pondurious. "Not all cared for him, and some even hated him. They had a very slanderous opinion of him. Maybe because his words made them trust less in themselves, which was frightening. Or perhaps they could never see beyond the rumor of his scandalous past. Even more so, perhaps it was because he was a challenge to their positions of wealth and power. But despite these people, who often made their negative opinions known, he had great compassion for all he encountered, even for those who disliked or hated him."

Felix commented, then questioned the sage, "I can certainly understand why some people must have liked him. It is even clearer why some may have hated him. However, please tell us, Pondurious, considering the reason we are here today, why are you speaking of him?"

Pondurious could see that perhaps interest was beginning to become muddled, so he continued by adding, "Of all the wonderful things he said and did which were perplexing and confounding, none was more puzzling than claiming to be the *Reason* and *Mission* of the *Why*. This claim of purpose and being had a way of evoking different responses. Some were troubled, while others were skeptical. But mostly, the majority were left perplexed and without a response. His closest friends, who were few, over time took it as an odd way of looking at oneself. They accepted him as being lovable, profoundly eccentric, and wise."

"Oh, come off it, Pondurious!" barked Rorke. "Where have we heard all this *Reason, Mission,* and *Why* nonsense before? Are you really trying to say that your so-called *building blocks of everything* was a man like you and me? This is a tale much too tall to believe!"

"As much as it is difficult for our professions to always see eye to eye, one representing the practical and the other science, I find your explanation of who this man is to be absurd!" added the scientist, Argon.

Then Felix cut into the protest, as if breaking up a quarrel. "Please, gentlemen! Your reputations are not at stake for trusting Pondurious. It is my neck on the cutting block for recommending Pondurious to speak to us. Even if he says the sun is the moon or the day is night, we have all agreed to hear him out."

Rorke and Argon said no more, facing Felix. Then Darius turned his eyes from the altercation to the sage. "Sir, my father is a wise, kind, and respectable man. I am highly insulted if anyone would imply he makes foolish decisions." The young man sternly gazed back at Rorke and Argon. Turning his face back towards the sage, he changed his expression and tone to a serious plea. "Sir, there is something inside of me that wants so much to hear more about this man. I believe you when you say he is exceptional, and I believe this is very important. Please tell us more about him. What is his name?"

The sage once again gave the young Darius an appreciative expression of endearment. After a short pause, Pondurious said, "His name is Gamgus."

"This is a most interesting name, Pondurious, " exclaimed Mayor Fredrick. "I'm not sure I have heard any name like it. Is it an old name?"

The sage replied, "Yes, it is very old, and for the people of the Primus Regions, it carries with it the meaning, *He is more than what he appears to be.*"

"This doesn't surprise me," said Rorke. "Much of what you have shared with us seems to be riddled with double meanings and very strange ideas."

"Much of life is like that, Rorke," the sage replied. "Too often we take for granted the profound things that are right in front of us. But rest assured, my recollection of the historic account of Gamgus and his friends will not fail to fill your minds and imaginations with thoughts that will elevate and bring a much-needed perspective. But for this to happen, it will require everyone to patiently and respectfully listen."

Pondurious did not disappoint. After hearing his recital of the timeline of existence, I was filled with awe and respect for this human named Gamgus. The pageant of the historical events still echoes inside of me today. I can still see every detail as clearly as when the human sage shared it with the crowd in my presence. It was both a terrifying and wonderful account indeed. Allow me the privilege to share it with you now.

Chapter 7 - Cave Number Seven

In a time and place many generations before Pondurious was born, there were many regions in the lands of this planet. The Primus Regions were united and governed by the committees of humans known as the Magistrates of the Primus Regions. These regions were divided by the very things that made each unique from the others.

The region called the Northern Primus Mountains spanned the areas where the foothills of the mountainous lands stretched across the continent. The mountains contained many slopes, cliffs, and caves, which were rich with minerals that all the regions used.

The region called the Primus Shores faced the salted water south of the Northern Primus Mountains. The human fishermen would draw water creatures from the salted water for food. Other valuable items were also caught and harvested from this salted water, which was called the ocean.

The region called Primus Medius was, as the name implies, the region that lay midway between the north and the south, which was between the Northern Primus Mountains and Primus Shores. This region was rich with good soil and farmland. It also was home to most of the humans, and they lived in close-knit villages and on small farms.

The size of all the regions combined would take travelers about six weeks on foot to cross from the shore to the south side of the mountain ranges. I once heard it said that my location is west, many weeks' journey across the great eastern ocean the mayor had made reference to.

The Magistrates of the Primus Regions were comprised of different ministries accountable to each other, all serving under this title. They all held sessions and operated in one of the small villages located in the Primus Medius region.

One such ministry, which ruled over all others, was the House of Magistrates. They were the humans who were responsible for the authoring and oversight of the laws in the regions. Their positions were decided by recommendations from every human. All regions would hold a contest for those picked based on their qualifications and good standing. Each region had two contest-selected representatives in the House of Magistrates serving the humans who lived in the towns, farms, and mountains.

There was also the Council of Magistrates, who were decided by contest as well. They would need to be approved by the House of Magistrates prior to candidacy in order to participate in the contest. The Council was more administrative and oversaw the ministries below them.

One of the ministries under the oversight of the Council of Magistrates was the Ministry of Geology and Land Mass Oversight. This ministry consisted of a handpicked and contracted head director by the Council of Magistrates. The head director of the GLMO, as it was called, was the human named Gamgus. Under his supervision and direction was a team of seven other humans. These humans were trusted servants who each had their areas of expertise to fulfill tasks that pertained to the ministry. They were also solicited positions, contracted, and handpicked by Gamgus.

Julius was the first of Gamgus's team of experts. His area of expertise was in soil analysis and mineral content. He was an older human whose skin was coarse and red due to many years being exposed to the elements. He was strong and tempered by formal training in recognition of rare earth minerals.

Then there was Stan. He had a narrow frame and was also advanced in years. He made up for it by being skillful in his ability to recognize and analyze the presence of dangerous liquids and gases. This was important so the team could navigate areas that posed dangers, ones that could lead to fire or explosions.

Lauren was the youngest human and newest member of the team. She was an attractive and very sturdy female human. Her area of expertise was cartography. Her skills went well beyond that, however. Not only was she an expert in mapping areas, but she was also a very talented graphic illustration artist. Her medium of choice was a Refined Carbon Scribe annotator, often referred to as an RCS. The RCS annotator was a brass tube device that contained a soft but stiff, thin carbon compound wick shaft. The carbon wick shaft could be moved forward by a sliding clip in a groove of the tube and locked in place. This would allow the wick to extend past the end of the tube, producing a writing tip. The RCS would produce a high-contrast fine black line that would execute well in diverse conditions. Being a very practical and diverse writing and drawing tool, it allowed a process called chemical cytography, which was a primitive method of printing copies from an original. Along with her maps, she would often be found doing sketches in her parchment book of the scenes and objects she encountered.

Cephus was not from the Primus Regions. His home was many months of human steps west beyond the Primus Mountains. His parents had fled to avoid wars among the neighboring tribes where he originally lived. They escaped when they were young and raised him while on their nomadic journey to find a settlement in the Primus Regions. He was very strong and had developed skills in rigging and tool management. These skills were very useful when the team needed to span chasms and scale mountainsides during expeditions.

Mark oversaw provisions, prepping, equipment inventory, and tool assistance. He, like the rest of the team, was fit and had proficient strength to endure the rigors of the environments they would often find themselves encountering. He was responsible for making sure food provisions were stocked and that any gear requiring maintenance was repaired. He had a well-versed background in food preparation, presentation, and preservation. He also had a working mechanical knowledge of the tools and equipment used by the team. He and Cephus would often be found working together to solve problems that crossed over into each other's area of expertise.

Hassan would be found working with Lauren. His skills centered around the trade of units and measurements. He was very diligent in recording and would take many notes about the specifics of his measurements so Lauren could transcribe them in her maps. His working knowledge of the devices he used demonstrated a precision that was necessary to the team's effectiveness. He was especially skilled in the use of the mechanical clinometer. He was a soft-spoken, strong, and tenuous human who did not speak out much in favor of quietly performing his duties.

Juan was also not originally from the area of the Primus Regions. His family originated from the southern lands located many human steps below the continent. The climate there was warmer, which gave his skin a darker hue than the rest of the team. He found himself in the Primus Regions when he met a female explorer who visited his land. They became a couple, and he returned with her to the Primus Regions, where she was from. He was well-educated in math—especially geometry—which made him very good at structural analysis and building. He and Cephus often worked together to solve problems and provide creative solutions for the rest of the team.

Over time, Gamgus and his team became like a kindred fellowship of family members. Their work took them to many places, and they were before people of many cultures. Because of his ability to interact with others and the confidence he demonstrated, this was the overriding reason why the man who claimed to be the *Reason* and *Mission* of the *Why* was contracted as the head of their department.

One day, they were commissioned to document and map cave number seven in a series of caves found in the foothills of the Calvert Mountains, located in the Northern Primus Mountains region. Cave number seven was located on the eastern side of the Northern Primus Mountains range, under the magistrate, the Honorable Helen Winwhisper. It was known that the caves contained valuable minerals and elements needed for life in those days. The electromechanical advancements and exploring techniques of today didn't exist then, so those tasks were done with basic tools, such as writing devices, parchment, mechanical clinometers, surveying scopes, and levels. Craftsmen made these objects out of wood, brass, copper, clay, and precious glass. Headlamps were of the liquid fuel and fire type. Charcoal and chalk keel devices, string, and rope were used to mark, level, and guide.

For cave number seven, they had packed a little over a day's worth of supplies, anticipating daily trips in and out of the cave. Mark oversaw the provisions needed for the exploration, one of which was the fuel to maintain the headlamps used for the exploration. Although everyone on the mission was trained for such an assignment, for some reason, there was nervousness in the air this day. Gamgus was the only one on the team not appearing to show any signs of being afflicted.

Gamgus was the first to approach the darkness of the opening of cave number seven, followed by his dedicated and loyal team. Stooping just in front, he stopped and turned to face them. "The mission we are about to undertake will not be without its challenges," he said to the team. "Lauren, I will need you to be drawing more than just the maps on this. It has been brought to my attention that you will also need to provide sketches of what occurs. I have it on the highest authority that we will be exceeding our scope of work."

"What authority are you referring to, Gamgus?" said Julius, who was the oldest and most seasoned of Gamgus's team.

"There is an authority that is above the Magistrates of the Primus Regions, Julius. Your loyalty is in the chain of command, and I have never given you any reason to doubt my leadership. You know this to be true since you have been with me from the very beginning my service to the Council of Magistrates."

"Yes, Gamgus," replied Julius, "but this is the first time you have ever made it known that you are deliberately acting outside of the scope of our work. How will the Council of Magistrates take to us diverting from the task we have been commissioned to do, and are we to be held accountable for doing so?"

"I have not said that we will be acting deliberately outside our scope, Julius. I have said that we will be deviating from it because of what will happen," replied Gamgus.

Mark inserted himself into the conversation. "Are you saying you know the future, Gamgus? We have witnessed you do some very strange and unexplainable acts, but you have never predicted the future."

Then Gamgus addressed everyone on his team, who were beginning to express signs of concern: "I cannot reveal to you why I know this to be true, but if I said nothing of my premonition, then you would not be on your guard. I can only ask you to trust me. It will all be made clear to you when the time comes."

The seven in Gamgus's team exchanged questioning glances. "Of course, we trust you, Gamgus. We are more than just contractors doing our job; we are also close friends," assured Julius. "We are ready to go."

As they entered the dark, rock-lined maze, which was lit by their dim headlamps and the ambient light from the now distant entrance, they began the tedious task of documenting and mapping. They meandered deeper through the winding chasms until the only light illuminating the pathway was from their carbon fuel lights on their heads. The sound of running water could be heard ahead. When they reached the source of the water, it was seen to be a small underground stream tracing the lower right side of the chasm they were following. It was not clear where the water source began or where it was headed. It was documented and added to the map as they continued to measure and record another footprint and cross-section of the underground maze formed long ago. They were deep in the cave when they began to feel and hear a low rumbling pulse and vibration under their feet, accompanied by the sound of water and stones cascading down.

"Cave-in behind us!" shouted Juan from the rear of the line. Realizing how close it was and coming from the direction they had entered from, all but Gamgus began to move at a frantic charge, deeper into the void and further from the way back.

Gamgus, now being left behind, shouted to the team, "Do not panic! It is okay! Slow down! There is no need for concern!" Slowly, the team began to realize they were leaving Gamgus behind. The now leaderless team began to slow down and return to the distant sound of his voice. Gamgus was calm and patiently waiting for them, like none of what was happening was of any concern. With a quiet and comforting tone, he said, "Do not be afraid. I am with you and will never let you go. I am faithful and true. If you trust and desire my guidance, all will work out well." For the first time, the others began to sense Gamgus was alien to them. Up until this event, they had all thought him strange and mildly conspiratorial, but now they were witnessing an assuring boldness in a crisis, beyond anything they had ever seen in him before.

"Are you not concerned about the cave-in that just happened behind us?" said Stan, who was catching his breath.

"We need to trace our steps back and see if the entrance is sealed off from us, Gamgus," Juan added.

"You can if you like, but I assure you that it is," Gamgus informed them. "But if you doubt me, then go investigate and report back to us what you find." Juan, who was now very concerned, gave a short nod and turned to backtrack to the location of the collapse.

When Juan returned, he reported to Gamgus and all the others, "It is completely sealed with no sign of daylight. The mass of the blockade is very dense. Because the supporting structure encompassing it appears to be very unstable, we can't risk removing it. I am afraid we have no choice but to seek another way out of here."

Gamgus's team was beginning to become very uneasy. "How did you know it would be blocked beyond hope, Gamgus?" asked Hassan.

"I have already told you that we will be deviating from our mission," replied Gamgus. "As I have tried to explain, the details are not clear to me. Nevertheless, we are destined to complete this mission, even if it is at great risk and cost."

"It appears that the only choice we have is to find another way out of here," Stan added, agreeing with Juan.

When they realized there was no pathway back, Gamgus announced, "We will continue with the mission as planned. If we do not continue to map and document, then we may find ourselves going in circles." The team all agreed. "We have a difficult journey ahead of us, so we will need all our strength to face what lies ahead. I think we should rest for a spell and eat."

Hassan must have been thinking to himself, *How could Gamgus be so certain of a difficult journey ahead?* I think it would be safe to conclude that the others must have been thinking the same thing.

When the others were preparing to settle down to eat, Mark took Gamgus to the side and informed him privately, "We only have enough food and provisions for just over a day. I would suggest we ration the portions to buy more time."

"Normally, I would agree with you, Mark," replied Gamgus. "But I am confident we will have all our needs met to complete this journey." Then, returning to the others, Gamgus announced, "We all need to eat until we are satisfied. Afterwards, we will need to rest." The others in the team all looked at Mark, then turned to Gamgus.

"I would agree with you, Gamgus," said Julius. "I think rest and proper nourishment are in order." Julius was looked upon as the second-in-command, so all the others took their seats on the ground.

It was true that they were exhausted and very hungry. Mark was worried because he was the one responsible for the provisions, and for the first time, he was finding himself doubting Gamgus. After they were finished eating, Gamgus said they should extinguish their lights and rest.

Hours later, they awoke from a surprisingly restful slumber. Each of the team members was strangely refreshed, and all seemed to have a positive attitude towards continuing their mission. Mark struck the flint of his headlamp to see how much fuel was left and if it needed a refill. To his amazement, he was able to make out that the fuel chamber was full, as if it had never been used. After lighting his headlamp, he opened the sack which contained the rations of food, and it was as if nothing had been eaten. *How could this be?* he thought to himself. He looked at Gamgus, who was just waking by the light from Mark's headlamp. Gamgus stretched his arms and, with a relaxed yawn, looked back at him with a pleasant smile. Mark was afraid to tell the others what he had discovered, so he kept silent as they woke and began to continue with their journey through the cave. He didn't want to face a confrontation with the team, who probably wouldn't believe him. The others did not realize what Mark knew and didn't think to check that their headlamps, which were still completely fueled.

Chapter 8 - The Song of the Mynerts

I will now pause before continuing with the human sage's story of Gamgus and his team. I am approaching where the events that are about to unfold become more fantastic, frightening, and mysterious. I will try to convey it as well as Pondurious delivered it to the gathering before him.

As they continued to work their way through the cave, Hassan recorded the direction and level of the path before them. The clinometer continued to show they were moving lower and lower. "Unless we start to trend upward, we are not likely to find another exit anytime soon," exclaimed Hassan to the others. It was easy to tell he did not like what he was seeing in his instruments. "We will need to find a cavern hosting a pathway to divert us upward. This will increase the odds of finding a way out of here."

"Don't lose heart, Hassan. The decision has been made, and truthfully, Gamgus is right… we really don't have any other option but to continue forward. We all need to remain positive and continue our mission by focusing on what we all do best," replied Julius. Gamgus gave an assuring smile at Julius. So, they continued the tedious process of measuring, taking samples, and recording information while working their way through the winding underground path.

Then the forward movement stopped. "This is most interesting." Julius had discovered a wall consisting of black rock containing a noticeably concentrated large area of pyrite. "Fool's gold," he said out loud to Gamgus and the others. The pyrite sparkled golden by the dim light from his headlamp, causing him to notice. As he began to probe the spot with his hand-held prospector's pick, the area of wall began to collapse. The team reared back from what appeared to be a wall of stone hiding an opening as it collapsed before them. The golden sparkle and gleam of the pyrite mixed with billowing black rock dust presented quite a spectacle. It was as if the opening was presenting itself as a glittering, magical drape being lowered while dematerializing before them. When the collapse had settled, Julius and Stan were the first to cautiously step through the opening, avoiding the jagged, sparkling rubble. The others followed behind them. Gamgus brought up the rear with Mark by his side.

"This is incredible," exclaimed Lauren with delight. She immediately pulled out her parchment book and began to sketch what she was beholding. They had stepped into a magnificent open cavern with limestone, stalactites, and stalagmites. It was as if they were transported into a new world with the beauty of a master's great work of art. Before them was an underground stream flowing into a small lake. As they approached the lake, the water was so still and black, the team's headlamps crafted a perfect mirror by which they could see themselves. They all stopped, as if in a trance, gazing at their own reflection.

All were captivated by the phenomenon until Juan noticed, in the reflection, directly above himself, a mosaic of chaotic bustling motion. He gasped. "What in the name of reason is this?" There, directly above them, were swirling, flittering shadows of many moving shapes on the ceiling. It looked like the pattern made by the eddies and swirls of water with hundreds of leaves caught tracing the currents. But these were not leaves in a pond. It was hundreds of creatures with small, dark grey featherless wings, quivering and bustling all at once from the disturbance of the visitors below them. As the flitter of wings bustled and collided, being provoked by the touch of the others, a hissing choral shrill of rodent-like voices began to grow, chattering and screeching like a flock of seagulls on the beach.

"Are you believing what you are hearing?" said Lauren.

"Are you believing what you are seeing" Juan answered her. All at once, the rest of the team looked up toward what sounded like small, high-pitched human voices. These sinister-sounding voices evoked emotions of fear and panic within their minds. The voices were projecting all at the same time, with many echoing cries of, *"Why have you come, Gamgus? Are you here to bring us to account?"* The team, being frightened and disturbed by this spectacle, all looked at Gamgus with troubled questioning expressions.

Lauren was the first to question Gamgus, voice raised over the chorus, "What are these creatures? Why are they calling out to you?" The team had all seen cave bats, but these were creatures of the likeness they had never seen. They had also never witnessed any creature who could communicate with human speech and provoke the emotions of fear they felt inside.

Gamgus turned to the team and said, "Don't be afraid!" He shouted over the crescendo of noise they were making. "They are mynerts, embodied followers of the fallen steward!" The others, who were crouching low in anticipation of an attack, looked into each other's eyes with terror. Only Gamgus stood straight and resolute with no appearance of fear in his expression.

"What nightmare of a creature is a mynert?!" Stan shouted over the wretched noise. "Who is this fallen steward you speak of?!"

Gamgus abruptly turned, facing all of them with a solemn and serious expression on his face. With a commanding, powerful summons, overriding the noise of the hideous creatures oscillating above their heads, Gamgus announced the name "Myrobah!" When the name left his lips like a warning, echoing in the cavern, the hundreds of mynerts began violently swarming and screeching with a terrifying noise over the panic-frozen team. What seemed like hundreds of high-pitched, tormented creatures in a choir, they began to cry out, "*It is he; it is he; it is he whom we serve. It is he; it is he; it is he whom we follow!*" While some were chattering, "*All that has been fashioned by the Why, Reason, and Mission will be surrendered!*" Others were heard screeching, "*We will rule with the great steward over all of his captured dominion!*" It was a terrifying crescendo of noise and chaos, growing louder and louder and more violently swirling over the heads of the team. The thick swarm of hideous creatures of the dark were descending, threatening to rip the flesh off Gamgus and his team's bones with their long, razor-sharp teeth.

Then Gamgus looked up, and with a low, thunderous roar, he shouted, "Be silent!" All at once, as if a flood of water overwhelmed a mighty fire, the great and horrifying spectacle of the hundreds of mynerts was quenched instantly. The mynerts all retreated to their perches in the cavern rocks, completely silent and still. Gamgus turned, calmly facing Hassan. "There is no threat here, Hassan. Please document everything that has happened to this point."

Hassan and the others were now stunned and staring at Gamgus in silence. "Y-yes, of course, G-Gamgus," Hassan stuttered.

"It is critically important that you recall as much detail as you can from the time that we entered the cave until this moment when the mynerts were silenced. Do this while it is fresh in your mind," said Gamgus. "From this point forward, take every opportunity to write down everything." Hassan nodded.

Then Gamgus turned to Lauren. "From this point forward, it is more important that you use your hidden talent as an artist to illustrate everything you experience. You have seen the sinister presence of the mynerts, so please draw a resemblance so others will know the terror they invoke. Also, draw the cavern and try to portray the beauty of it."

"Why are you asking this of us, Gamgus?" inquired Lauren.

"What is said and done in cave number seven, and continuing forward, must never be forgotten. Generations in the future will read and recall everything you will draw and write."

Hassan had a strange feeling upon hearing these words from Gamgus. This was not the first time he spoke as if he knew the future.

Mark began to ponder if he should tell Hassan about the food and headlamp fuel. But again, he couldn't find the courage to disclose it for the record.

"From this point forward, our mission for the Council of Magistrates is over. We are on a new mission now," Gamgus announced.

"What do you mean by a new mission, Gamgus?" asked Stan.

"This is a mission in which the scope goes beyond any purpose or cause that the Council of Magistrates could possibly require," Gamgus assured them.

"Have you been honest with us, Gamgus?" questioned Hassan. "How can you all of a sudden be saying this and not have known this all along?"

"I would have to agree with Hassan, Gamgus," added Julius. "One can't help but believe you have hidden this from us or that you are beginning to become mentally undone."

"My dear friends," said Gamgus, replying to the accusations, "I assure you that neither is true. I have known for many years that my purpose here on this planet was much more than my service to the Council of Magistrates. But I could never speak of it because I did not know the time or place of fulfillment. When we approached the cave,

I began to consider it would be here because there was an uneasiness I had never sensed before. When the cave collapsed behind us, I could feel the panic around me. I then began to look for affirmation but still needed to be silent about it. But finally, when we approached the wall of fool's gold and experienced the threatening, boastful song of the mynerts, I knew we were at the start of the fulfillment of my mission." His team all exchanged glances of cold and stunned silence. For as long as they had known each other, this was the first time they all felt as if they never even knew who Gamgus was. It was as if they were meeting him for the very first time.

The mynerts continued in their silence, as if under a captive spell. All that could be seen from the ground were hundreds of tiny black jewels of sparkling eyes affixed on them, refracting the dim lights of their headlamps. Gamgus, acting as if the Mynerts weren't there, turned to the team again and said it was time to rest and to eat.

Until then, no one had realized just how hungry they were. It was then that Julius remembered to check the fuel level in his headlamp. He had just remembered he hadn't approached Mark for any more fuel since they entered the cave. If the team did not maintain the lamps, it would be impossible to have vision in the cave. Almost in a panic, he reached for his headlamp to draw it down and check the level of fuel still left in it. *"How is this possible!"* he thought to himself. Now, looking around at the others, astonished and doubting what he was noticing, he spoke "We have been in this cave for almost two days. We should have filled our headlamps at least one time. I have just checked mine and have found it to be full!" The others all began to pull down their headlamps to examine them. Because of all the excitement and experiences that had happened, it never entered anyone's mind to do what was routine and keep the levels of their headlamps filled and operational. To their amazement, all the headlamps were completely full. Mark was the only one who was not surprised, but still he remained silent about what he already knew.

Gamgus and Mark, the only ones on the team who did not check their lamps, didn't seem bewildered by what one could call an impossibility. Lauren didn't notice Mark, but having her eyes on Gamgus, she noticed his reaction. "How is this possible, Gamgus? Please tell us what is really going on here. Many strange and unbelievable things have been happening, and now I am beginning to become very concerned and frightened."

Then Gamgus said something to Lauren and the rest of his team that was most troubling and strange. "You have, and will continue to witness many more occurrences such as this. All appearing impossible to believe. I can only ask you to continue with me. It will be difficult, and you may at times feel it is more than you can bear, but rest assured, you will find the strength and courage to bear it. Take comfort, for I will always be with you, even to the very end."

Then they nervously settled down, knowing the mynerts were overhead. Mark looked into the provisions bag, and once again it was full, as if he had just packed it. Again, he could not bring himself to tell the team what he was beholding. He thought to himself, *I must be crazy, and this must be a dream. This is an impossibility!* Once again, he looked over at Gamgus, but this time Gamgus did not smile back at him. His face was serious, as if he was sad and disappointed with him.

Then Juan began to think to himself, *there's not going to be much left to eat.* But Mark passed out full rations of bread, dried meats, honey, and mildly fermented juices, which were from the provisions they had packed for only one and a half days. Not knowing Mark had glanced down into his bag and saw it was still as full as when they had started, Juan asked Gamgus, "Will this be our last meal together?"

"Yes, Juan, my friend, it will be," said Gamgus to him. "But not for the reason of running out of food." Juan reared back, puzzled by this statement. The others had lost and bewildered expressions on their faces, reacting to what Gamgus just told Juan.

Gamgus, being the leader of the team, would always have a few words to say before all would eat. Sometimes he would thank the *Why* of all existence for providing. Other times it would be a reminder of challenges the team was facing and the appeal for wisdom in the *Why*. It was a very odd custom he had, and from time to time they questioned him, and this reference to the *Why*. He would try to explain it to them, but they had a hard time understanding. Perhaps he was merely expressing the mystery of the unknown, holding all the answers. It was his way to use a word to describe something difficult, if not impossible to fully comprehend. From time to time, any of them would talk to each other about it, only to come to the same conclusion. Julius would ask Gamgus about it, and Gamgus would reply, "All is under His dominion." Julius also asked Gamgus, "Why refer to the *Why* as a person?" But today was different because, for the first time, Gamgus did not thank the *Why* but thanked his father instead. The others looked back and forth at each other, taken aback from the change and not knowing what this meant. None of them really knew Gamgus's father. They had all met when they were adults, and although some spoke of their fathers, for the most part, this subject never came up.

Then they passed food to each other, breaking and dividing the portions, taking sips of the juices and silently, slowly, began eating. Juan lifted his eyes up to see the mynerts as still as leaves under the canopy of a great tree. Nervously, he looked down at the others, who also looked apprehensive, as if any minute the mynerts would erupt again. Gamgus was the only one who did not seem to be bothered by the unwelcomed guests with hundreds of refracting reptilian eyes staring at the gathering below them. When they were finishing up, it was time to clean up and continue. Gamgus broke the silence and said, "We have come a long way together, but now it is near time we should part. Many of you may be wondering what all this means, but I tell you it must unfold for you to understand." The others looked at Gamgus with concerned and puzzled expressions. Gamgus continued, "Let us establish a new meaning in this last gathering by celebrating the re-establishment of an era past." They looked at each other with questioning expressions, whispering back and forth to each other.

Stan leaned forward towards the others, saying, "Re-establishment of an old era? What does he mean? What is he talking about?"

Gamgus then announced, "The very world we live in will soon be undone, and all of the decay and sorrow we all live with will be no longer." More so than ever, a deep sense of fear of the unknown was beginning to overwhelm the team, who were at a loss for words. Gamgus then took the nearly empty container of the juice and some of the dried meat and held it up in the direction of the mynerts above them. With a loud voice, he proclaimed, "This declares the beginning of the end of the realm of the forsaken steward and his rule in the work of my father, which was once perpetual. Now is to begin the removal of the invoked curse by the law of entropy!" All at once the mynerts erupted into a violent swirl of hissing and speech, sounding like hundreds of small, shrill voices crying out, *"Show pity on us, Master of the perpetual! Leave us alone and return to the Why from where you were at rest!"* The mynerts, in a terrifying screeching whirl of chaos, began to disappear into the cracks and small fissures in the cavern walls until none were left. It was as though they had been sifted through the canopy of the cavern dome like it was a baker's sieve. Gamgus lifted his hands holding the food offering, and gazed into the gobsmacked eyes of his team. A loving and kind smile began to grow on his face, and he calmly spoke to his team. "All you love, and are called to love, will remember and know in this ritual that the enslavement of the realm of the fallen steward will be forever abolished." Gamgus then began to drink and eat the dried meat, passing it to the others who joined with him. All their years together, this had never been done before. They all had been driven by hunger and had eaten till they were satisfied. It was out of the ordinary to be consuming another meal after they were all full, but they were driven by a strange sense of purpose and destiny. No one understood why they felt this way, but Gamgus would later reveal it to them. When they were finished, Mark looked into his bag, which was now nearly empty. Instead of reacting in fear of running out of food, he had a strange sense that this would not be his last meal. As was the case before, he kept this information to himself.

Chapter 9 - The Great Waterfall

When the team had finished the meal of juice and dried meat, Mark collected all the empty containers and stowed them away. Gamgus rose first and announced to the others, "It is now time to continue our journey." He slowly began to walk in the direction of the mirrored underground lake. The rest of the team gathered their wares and slowly followed behind him. When he stepped into the lake, the water came up to his knees. The mirror was transformed into ripples of dancing colors from the shattered reflections lit by their headlamps. It was as if he had stepped into the other side of a mirror world, disrupting its reality. He then slowly turned to his team, who had stopped moving towards him. The others looked at each other while Mark entered the water to join Gamgus. The others slowly and cautiously began to move forward, joining the pair. They were moving towards what sounded like an underground waterfall. The bottom of the lake was as smooth as the surface had previously been.

Juan thought to himself, *This is a very odd and unnatural geological formation. Such a smooth and perfect surface existing below the water in the depths of a cave.* He had studied stone formations and contours formed by water, and they would always have random variations in texture, containing rocks and other foreign particles. But the surface below his feet was smooth like a slate drawing board and not at all slippery. The footing was firm and stable, like a rough-textured sanding stone. They walked for about one mile until they approached a great underground waterfall.

"Oh my!" Lauren gasped at the sight, and she reached for her parchment sketchbook and began to draw what was before her. The others stood mesmerized by the size and beauty of the great wispy tail of water. The ceiling of the cavern was almost one hundred feet high, looming ominously above them. From the top of the ceiling, the great pillar of water emptied itself from the opening with a majestic force, fanning into a misty white column, blissfully descending with a soft roar.

Julius gave Stan a puzzled look. "Such an uncanny phenomenon. The water from the falls doesn't seem to be disturbing the mirror below it."

"It also appears the noise is coming from the fall and not the sound of it striking the mirror of the lake. It is as if it defies the laws of nature," added Stan.

Gamgus stood before the great column of descending water. The roar was a steady, continuous tone like a magnificent wave breaking continuously on an ocean shore. Gamgus turned and said to the others, "Follow me." He then turned back, facing the great waterfall with arms stretched wide. Moving forward, as if his intention was to embrace the column of the downward turbulence, something happened as he was entering the great wispy downpour.

The roar of the great waterfall began to form words in a loud, static-embedded voice. It echoed in the great cavern, overwhelming and terrifying them as it proclaimed, *"I am the Why, and before you are the Reason and the Mission. The Reason and the Mission share equality in Me. Each of us is separate yet all united. We exist in perfect relationship, and We are One. I sent the Reason so you will know Us through the Mission. The Mission shall be with you always. The Reason stands before you to bring with Him the Mission, and in Him I am satisfied. Desire, trust, and follow Him."*

The others were all shaken to the core by the soul-penetrating words, which sounded like ocean waves breaking on the shore. Gamgus continued forward as the water emptied over him. He slowly disappeared into the falls and was seen no more by the stunned remaining team.

It was Mark who broke the silence. "What just happened?" Trembling, he turned to the others and said, "Did he say for us to follow him?" In fact, it was true that Gamgus did say to follow him, and it was also true that the phenomenon of the voice from the falls said the same.

Juan reasoned Gamgus must have walked through what was an opening to another area. It was hidden, the waterfall acting as a great curtain. Even though they were all still in a state of shock by the spectacle, Juan was the first to find the courage to move towards the great veil of water. It was a strange sense of bravery he began to feel as he remembered the voice of the falls and Gamgus asking them to follow.

Lauren was concerned about her sketches and placed her book into her backpack. She knew it was constructed to resist water. She proceeded with haste through the waterfall, yet carefully, to avoid getting soaked any more than needed.

Cephas held tight to his ropes and rigging tools and barreled through the concealed opening.

Hassan made a few final feverish notes in his book, describing the size of the area and his best guess at the size of the opening. He also wrote down the words of the voice, which came from the white noise of the waterfall. Like Lauren, he too placed his book into his backpack and hurried through the passage.

Stan and Julius followed right behind him.

Mark was the last left behind. He found it very odd that the others seemed to just brush off what was nothing short of an impossibility. Mark, unlike the others, found it to be more difficult to move forward. He decided to address the phenomenon of the waterfall. "Who is the voice we just heard speaking from the falls?" Being the last one left, he waited, only hearing the sound of falling water.

After a long pause, the voice spoke to Mark, "*I am the voice of the Why.*"

Mark, terrified and all by himself, was once again left with the choice to disclose to the others the unbelievable thing that was happening. He had asked the falls a question and it had answered him! Finding the courage, he replied to the voice of the falls, "What awaits me on the other side of the falls?"

Then the voice of the *Why* in the falls answered, *"Why are you afraid, Mark?"*

Mark was now undone. The voice knew his name and his feelings. He had no doubt this voice knew his thoughts. "How can I help but be afraid? The others have not witnessed the many things I have seen that are impossible. Even now, *this* is impossible!"

"For me, Mark, nothing is impossible," the voice from the falls replied.

Mark was now emboldened to reason with the voice from the falls. "The others had no problem blindly following Gamgus through the falls. They were not aware of all that I had witnessed. This is why I believe even greater things await, and what lies on the other side will be more than I can bear."

The voice of the *Why* spoke again. *"You are correct, Mark. It will be more than you can bear. But for that reason, you must face your fears so that what is of greater importance may be obtained."*

What possibility could wait on the other side? Mark thought to himself, even more overwhelmed by fear. But then he remembered Gamgus said to follow and that he would be able to bear it. Was the voice from the falls lying to him? It was his trust in Gamgus that was now giving him the courage to face his fear and giving him the will and desire to plunge into the mystery of the great waterfall.

The young man named Darius interrupted the sage, Pondurious. "This is an incredible accounting, Pondurious! How did Mark face his fears? If I were in his situation, I don't think I would have the courage to go through the falls."

Pondurious, with a kind smile, said to the young Darius, "No one may ever be able to understand why a human heart finds courage. But it is evident to me that because he heard the words of Gamgus, he found that courage. It is important to realize that courage comes from outside the universe of one's own being."

"But how could Gamgus be telling the truth and the *Why* tell a contradicting truth if they are one? Wouldn't one be lying?" asked Darius.

The sage answered him, saying, "You will see that often the truth is found after all is revealed. I will allow you to decide the answer to your question when I finish my account of the events that unfolded."

At this point of my recollection of Pondurious's account, I was at a loss for words. This sage was speaking of something that was far more mysterious and from before my time. *"Outside of the universe of my own being?"* I thought to myself. I am a well of ancient origins. I have no point of reference from the first thought I ever had to comprehend this. But even so, the story told by the sage filled me with the desire to hear more. It is still as fresh in my mind as my water used to be.

Chapter 10 - The Cathedral of Myrobah

Despite the day beginning to grow long, the audience of humans before me was still captivated by the ancient saga the sage was recalling. The detail and the way that he presented it were beautifully recited, as if it were a fine play or musical performance.

One might wonder how this sage had such a clear and vivid recollection with such precise detail. Later, I would discover that he had told it many times and was able to remain consistent and fluent. My very nature as a well allows me to recall perfectly. I experience everything that happens to me and around me. I cannot say why this is my nature, but it appears to be a talent, or for lack of a better word, "gift." Although I appear to possess this "gift", I had no idea who might be the gift-giver. Allow me the privilege to continue reciting the sage's retelling of the history, exactly as I heard him tell it.

As the rush of the great waterfall curtain produced the emerging, soaked last member of Gamgus's team, Mark saw the others with Gamgus, fixated on the incredible panorama in front of them. The cavern on the other side of the great waterfall looked like a crude bronze-colored cathedral of stone with iron ore embedded in the stones. The opening they passed through, now behind them, looked like a tall, jagged window frame. The white cascading water behind the frame backed the outline, creating a mock stained glass. It was as though the falls had cut the shape, but on the other side of the mock glass veil, the beauty of the opposing side was lost. The great cathedral was ugly and dark, with very little light. No one remembered to extinguish their headlamps, but the force of the water that bore down on them from the great water veil saw to it. The light in the immense cavern cathedral was produced by low-lit, irregular sconce pockets of burning coals, giving the room a dark, blood-red glow. The red glow gave the falling torrent mock stained glass window a ghostly salmon-tinted color. The water below their feet was no longer dark, still, cool, and reflective, like a mirror. It was now a sickening, pea-green color, giving off a chemical, pungent, foul odor.

"This water feels acidic, and I smell burning sulfur," commented Stan.

Ahead of them was a great mound of the same pyrite-infested black rock Julius encountered when he uncovered the entrance past the cave-in. The rock pile towered at least thirty feet and had a base extending out like a large platform. The pyrite reflected the dull glow of the deep-red light filling the room. It produced a low red-gold glimmer, which might have been considered beautiful if not for the surrounding ambience of the room.

Lauren reached for her backpack and retrieved her parchment sketchbook. She was able to strike the flint of her headlamp and relight it. *"This is the most unusual interior I have ever witnessed in all my days of exploring. This is certain to be the work of intelligent designers, but using very crude means. Truly amazing but deeply menacing at the same time*, she thought. As the warm glow of her headlamp struck the pages, she began to nervously sketch what she was observing. On the page she began to sketch a huge cavern, which she later titled "The Great Gothic Cathedral."

Not long after Lauren began work on her sketch, the great underground cathedral was filled with a familiar noise. From the many irregular edges and fissures in the dark, bronze-looking rock walls, dark gray, reptilian, winged creatures the size of large cave bats began to spill out into the room. Like the sound of jungle leaves being moved violently by an incoming tropical storm, hundreds of mynerts burst forth into the great cathedral, colliding into the walls and each other. Adding to the noise of their appearance was a high-pitched screeching, like a frenzied choir, each singing and saying different things. Then, all around the team's feet appeared a violently swirling dark current of slithering, half-blind cave eels. The eels began to wrap and entwine themselves around their ankles, constricting them so they could not walk, holding them in place. Gamgus remained still, calm, and fixed while the others began to struggle, experiencing terror and panic.

"What is the meaning of this!" shouted Julius.

"These dreadful eels have me held in my place. I can't move!" added Stan over the noise from the mynerts.

"What will become of us, Gamgus!" was the panicked plea from Lauren.

Then, in front of them, the great slithering school of cave eels began to part, creating an opening in the sick green water. Out of the opening rose a giant creature, like a beast surfacing for air, a sight none of the team would ever forget.

"What in the name of all dark nightmares is this?" cried out Juan.

It was a monstrous, blindfolded cave olm at least a hundred times the size of any olm ever documented. The great olm was terrifying but also very magnificent. It was as if you were looking at a small insect under an extremely powerful magnifier. From a distance it may appear harmless and not much of a threat, but under a very powerful magnifying glass it takes on the form of a wild beast with great mysterious features and body parts unfamiliar and unlike anything known on the planet.

As the mynerts were swarming over the heads of the team, they began to shriek in waves of unison, *"Why are you here, Gamgus?"* They spoke in a high-pitched chatter, like a swarm of mighty locusts. *"No one dares enter the great hall of sacrifice. For so doing makes them our captives to torture and consume! We cannot touch you, Gamgus, but those you have brought are ripe and savory gifts we will offer to the great fallen steward! Your dearest friends will be no more, and you will be left all alone!"* As the mynerts raged in their frightening chorus of impending doom, their threatening continued to intensify. They began swooping down and striking the team as the swirling great knot of eels below their feet constricted even tighter.

With their wide, gnashing mouths and long, serrated teeth, they descended on the team. Lauren screamed out, "They're going to devour us!" The others in the team had also reached a level of panic that had them howling and thrashing as the assault intensified. They were all fearing for their lives except for Gamgus.

Gamgus was the only one who stood tall and resolute, and a superhuman noise, as if blown from a mighty trumpet, blasted out of him as he with great authority bellowed the name, "Myrobah!"

All at once the slithering constrictors at their feet released and the eels began to recede. The mynert swarm above them began to gust back and forth, swooping away from the team and fixing themselves to the cavern ceiling. When all was settled, there was complete silence. Then Gamgus addressed the great monstrous olm, Myrobah, "You know why I have come."

Much to the shock of the rest of the team, Myrobah replied with a forceful and low, soul-penetrating voice. "You have come to break the chains that bind all, but there is only one thing which can accomplish it. This one thing is hidden from me." The walls of the great cathedral acted as an amphitheater and caused his voice to be sustained monstrously and with the illusion of power. Myrobah, with a sinister and pleased menacing tone, continued, "*Reason* and *Mission* of the *Why*, although my eyes are covered, I smell your presence. My plan of your defeat is now before me, for I believe you are now powerless. You have been made weak because the only hope to save your friends is to surrender to me. You have failed to realize becoming human made you subject to me, giving me power over you."

Mark, in his terror, thought to himself, *what does he mean by declaring that Gamgus had become human?* The others were all speechless, glancing at each other with expressions of deep and perplexed fear.

Stan looked at Julius, then said, "Who or what was he before becoming human? This is all beyond my ability to comprehend and accept."

They all had known Gamgus for many years and had never considered him to be of any other origin than a normal man. His leadership qualities were simply part of his nature, but up until now, no one had been confronted with the real reason for this. Gamgus was always confident and the words he spoke when making decisions or commenting were profound and wise. He never seemed to find himself embroiled in conflict with other people. He had enemies but he always treated them with words and actions geared towards reconciliation and not retaliation. It was now dawning on all of them that his identity, and reason for his existence, had been kept a secret.

Then Gamgus answered Myrobah, "In all matters, the *Why*, *Reason,* and the *Mission* was, is now, and will always be. What is fashioned from this perpetuality is sustained by the natural cause and effect of this truth. But as you have rightly concluded, it is this relationship maintained by the will which is broken by the same. In your pride and blindness, caused by the beauty and power of your given nature, you will never be able to see this. Rather than the gratitude and trust one would have by embracing the revealed *Reason* and *Mission*, you have rejected this and have made a lie your truth instead. Because this is your blind will, you have severed this relationship and have chosen enmity against your very origin. You have risen in your self-deceived praise and believe you are greater than the source of your origin!"

At these words, Myrobah began to laugh as if he had caught Gamgus in a trap. He knew Gamgus had placed his very existence into the hands of a captured universe. Best of all, the fallen and lost had captured subjects of the very work the *Why* had fashioned in His own image. Myrobah knew he could do anything with what had been turned over to him. He spent many years seeking to propagandize and persuade humanity to turn their backs on the source of their origin. He believed it would be the final blow to the great *Why* if his beloved *Reason* and *Mission* were destroyed. Surely the *Why* could not survive being separated forever from the beloved *Reason* and *Mission*. If the person of the *Reason* died, then certainly the person of the *Mission* would follow. Now, for the first time, he was certain it was in his reach, and what happened next was all Myrobah had hoped for.

Gamgus then spoke again to Myrobah, "It is the will of my father that I offer myself to you in exchange for the lives of my team and all the enslaved. Only I can give this to you. It is not yours to take. I am here to settle what is owed and what can only be paid by one who is not subject to the law of entropy. Because I and my Father are one, the *Reason* is being revealed by the *Mission* of the *Why*."

At these words, the dim red sconces of burning coal began erupting in violent flames. The water below Gamgus and his team began to grow hot, and the eels entwined themselves around their ankles once again. "Now feel the strength of my servants at your feet. They obey my commands!" bellowed the raspy, ominous-sounding voice of Myrobah. No one could move, and as the team struggled, all but Gamgus fought to break free.

The mynerts began their shrieking descent to attack once again, but this time they focused on Gamgus. The eels at Gamgus's legs began to bite him and bright red pools of blood billowed in the water below his knees. *"We are grateful for this delicious meal, Oh Great One!"* the mynerts above them chattered in high-pitched shrieks. *"His flesh will satisfy our hunger!"* The swarm of mynerts came down like a great hailstorm, striking Gamgus and ripping small pieces of his flesh until it became hard to recognize him. He was becoming a silhouette of a man, a mangled bloody figure, right before the eyes of his team, who were being held by the eels.

"Stop it! Stop it!" cried Lauren, who now had great tears in her eyes.

One would have to wonder…if the eels did not detain his team from running to his rescue, then most assuredly, the horror of what was happening before them would have paralyzed them anyway. It was like watching a horrible, violent accident, which happens quickly but is perceived as going in slow motion.

Myrobah began to laugh, which filled the great cathedral in a slow crescendo, building to a roar. "Pathetic images of the *Why*, *Reason*, and *Mission*, who are now becoming worthless tools of my pleasure! I so enjoy hearing the tormented wailing coming from each of your weak voices as my servants torture and mutilate your only hope!"

The mynerts began to join in the swelling laughter with satisfied shrieks of delight, proclaiming, *"Gamgus is now ours and our day has come!"* The sconces of fire blazed higher and higher. Gamgus, being the closest, was now beginning to burn. The sight was more than the team could stand to watch, and they began to cry out to Myrobah for mercy for their dear friend's sake.

Myrobah continued his laughter, the sound filling the cavern like rolling thunder. "Fear not, my desperate subjects!" sarcastically he addressed the seven. "I will spare you and cherish your pathetic sobbing. But I will never forget the loyalty you have shown for the one I am consuming before you. You will live but will surely come to know the worst in me for it!"

Yet Gamgus stood resolute, despite what must have been agony, and miraculously kept silent. His arms were outstretched to the sides like a scarecrow in a field facing a swarming flock of pecking and mocking crows. No one at this point could believe he was still alive and was enduring the most grotesque and brutal torture a human being ever had to endure. The mynerts continued to descend on him, and now pieces of bone could be seen as the flesh was stripped away. None of the others would have ever survived what was the worst display of mutilation and burning alive they could have ever imagined. Then, after what seemed like an eternity, the attack and laughter ceased. Gamgus, who now vaguely resembled a human form of bone and burnt, shredded flesh, laid open from head to toe, slowly lowered his arms and bowed his head. To the shell-shocked amazement of his team, he slowly exhaled, speaking his final words. "The needed work is done. Father, I surrender to you." He then slowly sank to a crouch. But instead of rolling forward, he gently laid himself back into the water, surrendering his life as if preparing for a never-ending deep sleep.

The surrounding eels formed a current supporting the motionless corpse of the team's loyal friend. The eels rafted the now dead and mutilated body of Gamgus towards the altar of Myrobah. Myrobah had a great greedy expression of satisfaction on his slimy, blindfolded olm face. His massive and hideous arms reached down and picked up the grossly disfigured body of Gamgus and laid it on the altar below his cracked and slimy feet. Rancid yellow drool seeped from his crooked smile, which hosted long and irregular sharp teeth. Then Myrobah began to speak with an amplified tone of dark, sick joy. "Let it now be known the power and glory of all the *Why*, *Reason*, and *Mission's* dominion are now mine. No longer can the universe and all of humanity serve each other, but only through me and all I represent. You are now blind masters of your own path. The path you choose is one of the many only I can offer. You will only serve me, and your fate will be decided by me alone. Now you see your disobedience will end in a place much like the fool lying before you. If I am pleased with you, then you will rule those who I am less pleased with. Never forget I am your master, and you will serve only me. Your fate is now sealed to the law of entropy, and you will live until your flesh is found in absolute dark atrophy. But it will not stop there, my enslaved subjects. Forever your disembodied consciousness, the only evidence of *His* sickening treasure remaining will be in absolute dark and isolated torment by the inner voices only you will hear in the energy of your enslaved soul!"

The sorrow and distress of the team felt like it was beyond their ability to bear. It was Cephas who was the first to have enough courage to respond to Myrobah, who seemed to be anticipating a response. With his head held low and despair in his voice, Cephas pleaded, "Please, terrifying, fierce, and powerful one, may we depart from here and take the remains of our friend to see to his final resting place?"

Myrobah only scolded him with words, disparaging his timid request for sympathy. "Stupid, senseless fool! The remains of Gamgus are mine and they will be my trophy that will be a witness of my power!" Myrobah then spoke again, proclaiming to the team, "I show no mercy except for what serves my purpose. Behold before you!" Then the great thirty-foot altar of pyrite-infested rock began to shake and rumble. Great black dust clouds began to roll and swirl from the inevitable collapse of black sparkling rock while the Mynerts began to chatter and click with excitement. The great Olm stepped off the altar and faced it while the shredded and bloody remains of Gamgus laid before the great quaking wall of billowing black dust and glitter. The glowing red sconces of hot coals began to swell with sparks and fire as the refracting pyrite shimmered by the movement. Myrobah once more began to rise with a roar of laughter. The great thirty-foot wall collapsed, forming an avalanche of cascading pyrite-laced rock falling and crushing the mutilated remaining body parts of Gamgus. The team stood paralyzed, grief-stricken at the sight of their dear friend's body being completely entombed by the violent display. Lauren clutched hold of Mark for comfort as the tears of terrified, dread-filled sorrow fell from her eyes. It was a clear and deliberate proclamation of the cruelty of Myrobah and a final declaration he forever held the remains of Gamgus.

When the show of crushing rock, fire, and black dust was over, the settling dust slowly revealed a great opening in place of the absent wall behind the altar, just as the great waterfall hid the entrance of the cathedral. The altar of Myrobah hosted a great mound of rock, which was now the tomb of Gamgus. Myrobah turned to face his terrified guests with a content and sinister smile as he guarded his precious trophy. Then Myrobah spoke his final words to Gamgus's devastated and broken-hearted team. "And now, depart from this place and tell all others what you have seen. Tell them all hope for the universe, the planets, and humanity will no longer reflect a once perpetual goodness. The great, fierce, and powerful steward of the *Why, Reason,* and *Mission* now rules forever the realm of decay and atrophy. I now rule this order containing all evidence of the realm of the *Why* until all is ended and all hope in the perpetual ceases to exist. I will have the great pleasure of continually reminding the *Why* in his pride and power that He created His own despair. His pain will be so great he will regret what he ever loved. From this point forward, the great truth on your planet will be the realm of Myrobah and those loyal to me!"

Being crushed, demoralized, and not having the power to fight, the team collected themselves and moved towards the newly formed opening. The sorrow, loss, bewilderment, and fear they all felt could not be mistaken in the countenance on their faces and their posture as they moved towards the exit. Myrobah'sminions began to mock them and laugh.

"Pathetic creatures of the once mighty Why, Reason, and Mission!" snarled the mynerts in waves. *"We take great pleasure in watching them suffer!"* said others. *"Where is your dominion over the great one now?"* they said even more, while the wicked, blindfolded face of Myrobah followed the soul-tortured sound and smell of the surviving seven leaving.

They passed the great mound entombing the remains of Gamgus and went through the opening. They could hear the celebratory sounds of the mynerts decreasing as they traveled further away. After what seemed like miles, the clicking noises of the sinister jubilation diminished to nothingness. Despite all the shock and trauma of what happened, they continued to document and map the cave exit and write down all they could remember of what was said and done before them. A sober sense of loyalty and dedication to their lost friend strangely empowered them to have the courage to continue. Despite the sorrow and tears, they all fought; Juan, Hassan, Lauren, and all the others worked to finish the task given to them by Gamgus and the Council of Magistrates. They all had a strange sense that this was what Gamgus would have wanted them to do. Then, at last, a small amount of sunlight could be seen ahead. The overwhelming weight of their sorrows and worries became a little lighter when they crossed the threshold into the sunlight outside of cave number seven.

Chapter 11 - Expedition for the Council of Magistrates

When they found themselves outside the exit of cave number seven, Juan placed markers so the opening could be easily located. Soon after, Juan recognized a familiar landmark and was able to reconcile their location. They traveled along the perimeter of the mountains towards the direction of the other side of cave number seven. The team was exhausted, both mentally and physically, and it was beginning to grow dark. They knew they had at least a five-mile journey on foot just to reach the point at which they had originally entered the cave, but it was the most direct way back to town. They hoped they would be able to cut some distance short by finding an alternative landmark in the morning. From their original entrance of cave number seven, it would be a five-to-ten-mile walk back to the edge of town.

Mark investigated the remaining food provisions and saw there was very little left. "We should only drink water tonight to ensure we have enough rations to make it back to town tomorrow." Stan and Julius gathered some firewood, and the team pitched camp for the night.

Before they all retired, they gathered around the campfire, a troubled silence engulfing them. It was Mark who broke the silence. "I hadn't told anyone until now, but the food supply was miraculously replenished in the cave. I kept it to myself because I thought everyone would think I was crazy."

"After what we have just been through, I certainly don't believe you are," assured Julius.

"No one blames you for that, Mark. If we hadn't just witnessed all the events that occurred afterwards, we *would* have thought you were crazy," Hassan said with a halfhearted chuckle. Everyone gave Mark a kind, assuring smile, one of acceptance.

Mark nodded while looking down, still saddened by his lack of courage. Looking up at the others, he added, "I know you all believe me, but I am concerned that the Council of Magistrates may not be so accepting."

Lauren, who was making some last-minute enhancements on one of her drawings, spoke without looking up. "Yes, it is difficult even for me to believe the pictures I am crafting. But I cannot deny what I saw, and I know in my heart the images I am drawing capture well what I witnessed."

"The good news is that we *all* experienced what had happened so it will be difficult for the Council of Magistrates to doubt our story," added Cephas. "But still, remembering what I saw, we have more than just how unbelievable it is to overcome."

"I think the biggest problem we will face is the absence of Gamgus," added Stan.

Dead silence, save for the crackle of the fire, met with the darkness surrounding them, overcame the conversation.

"Nevertheless," Julius broke the silence, "we need to tell the truth and let the consequences go where they may. What we have witnessed is beyond anything ever experienced and the importance of a full record of events is critical. The implications go far beyond our ability to comprehend, and we should have the resolution that everything depends on it."

"I think it would be a good course of action to convince the Council of Magistrates that we should return to Myrobah's cathedral as soon as possible with an expedition team. Perhaps we could still recover Gamgus's remains for a proper burial and put to rest any concerns," suggested Hassan.

"It may also be a good idea to not yet mention the great olm to the Council of Magistrates. We should wait until we return to the place where Gamgus lies," said Mark.

Then Lauren burst out, "That name, Myrobah, is the most offensive sound on this planet!" A defiance was beginning to grow in her heart. "How dare he say such things to us like we were caged animals! I will never forget the torture he and his minions inflicted on Gamgus. If there were any possible way, I would see to it that he suffers the same demise!" But then, as if a dark and desperate reality overcame her, she broke down sobbing, covering her face with her hands, overwhelmed with despair. Juan rushed to her side and put his arm around her to comfort her. She was beginning to grieve the loss of Gamgus.

"It was profound wisdom that Gamgus instructed us to continue our mapping of the cave. It will be useful in navigating the expedition back," Stan said after Lauren began to calm down. Everyone solemnly nodded in agreement to all that was discussed. They all wondered to themselves if the great olm would still be there when they returned.

Having settled all things for the time being and deciding to come back with the expedition crew, the team finally fell asleep. Silence now occupied the camp, only broken by the faint sounds of the wind, forest creatures, and the dying crackles and pops from the dwindling campfire. Except for Lauren, the rest of the team hadn't even had a chance to mourn the loss of their leader and friend. They were only able to sleep for as long as it was dark. The summer nights were shorter, so their sleep was brief, restless, and shallow. After being woken by the first sign of light, they arose and began their journey back to report to the Council of Magistrates. Gamgus was the leader and part of his responsibility was to be a trail guide. He had a talent for following marks and positions of constellations. It took a combined effort from the rest of the team to plot and follow the pathway back in his absence. They followed along the foothills for about four miles until they found the entrance of the collapsed side of the cave. No alternate landmark was discovered to shorten their journey back. Once they made it to the entrance of cave number seven, the path back to town was clear. It wasn't until late into the night that they made it back.

When they entered late the hall of the Council of Magistrates, they were welcomed back by the night shift acting representatives of the council. The team was tired, hungry, and very dirty. The task of mapping a cave was known to be a very grimy, physical job. It was not long before Sir Aaron, who was one representative of the council, first noticed that Gamgus was not with them. "Where is Gamgus, Mark?"

"I have most devastating news, Sir Aaron. Gamgus was killed in cave number seven by a most dreadful collapse." Mark thought to himself that his answer was clever, hoping it would avoid any questions about the unbelievable spectacle leading up to the avalanche of rock. After all, no one could really be certain if it was the torture of the creatures of Myrobah or the crushing rock that killed him. But despite this obfuscation of the facts, Mark felt guilty, having a strong conviction that Gamgus drew his last breath after he said, *"The work is complete."*

Sir Aaron winced at the horrible news. Overhearing the conversation, Councilman Sir Eustis, who had been speaking to Julian, quickly turned his attention and advanced towards Mark and Sir Aaron. "What is this I am hearing, Mark? Please elaborate."

"Well, sir, you see…um." They had all agreed not to tell the whole story. Mark could not say that Gamgus was mutilated by a swarm of talking creatures called mynerts, which were unknown to the council. Not to mention, a giant, hideous, blindfolded cave olm who caused an avalanche of rock to crush and entomb his body.

But Lauren couldn't allow Mark to maintain this charade, and despite what the team had decided, she began to erupt once again, out of emotion, "Gamgus suffered a most horrible and violent execution from a vile beast named

Myrobah in his demented cathedral of stone! He now lies in a rock tomb, which that deplorable beast fashioned like a memorial trophy!" Juan rushed to her as she was sobbing again, attempting to calm her down. She pushed him aside angrily, having nothing to do with his attempt to comfort her. Sheepishly reeling back, Juan realized his mistake. He was now seeing the strength she was demonstrating in her weakness.

Sir Aaron laughed nervously. "Obviously we need to consult Stan to see if some strange odorless gas was causing one of your teammates to hallucinate, Julius." turning to him.

Lauren looked at all the others who now had betrayed looks on their faces. She gave them all a contemptuous frown, glaring them down.

"I assure you, Sir Aaron, this is no matter to make light of. You need to apologize to Lauren for your inappropriate response," Julius responded with irritation.

"I don't see how it is inappropriate, Julius," retorted Sir Aaron. "She is describing things that could only exist in lore and is void of reality. Either she was hallucinating, or she has lost her mind."

"She is speaking the truth, Sir Aaron," Stan interjected, emboldened and concurring with Lauren, despite how it might affect his reputation. "Even if there was some invisible gas—though my expertise determined that there was not—it wouldn't explain that we all saw the same thing."

Lauren looked appreciatively at Stan and Julius for standing with her. "Thank you, Stan, and thank you, Julius," she said to them. "I know that took a lot of courage." She glared at the others in turn. Even though they had all agreed to not speak of it, she stopped at Mark with a betrayed, angry look on her face.

"Is this story true, Julius?" said Sir Eustis, now deeply troubled.

Julius looked down as if being caught in the act, then up at the others, who slowly began to nod their heads in agreement. "Yes, Sir Eustis, I am afraid so."

Seeing that the others were all in agreement, Sir Eustis said, "Well, that *is* something, Julius. Something indeed."

"Yes! Something indeed, Julius," parroted Sir Aaron. "Either you and your team are telling the truth or, more likely, are embroiled in some sinister cover-up."

Mark, now finding his courage, snapped at Sir Aaron, "Meaning no disrespect, but certainly we would have made up a more believable story if that was the case."

Still, their story and the fact of the whole team concurring did not convince Sirs Aaron and Eustis, who represented the council. But one thing they could all agree on: Gamgus was not with them. This fact alone was enough to convince the council to send an expedition of forces to find and retrieve the remains of a confidant who was also an asset to the Council of Magistrates. It was especially important that all those who were close to Gamgus found closure. If the story about his death were true, it would be improper and disrespectful to not ensure verification of what had happened, and especially, a proper burial. So, it was decided by the council that the remaining members of Gamgus's team—Julius, Stan, Mark, Hassan, Cephus, Lauren, and Juan—would depart early the next day with a crew of specialists and excavators.

Present in the expedition team were the town's coroner, Servia, and her assistant, Mendel, to confirm his death and the cause thereof. Servia was trained in the art of the human body but was not certified to practice as a physician who would tend to the sick. Her skills in human anatomy served to certify death and prepare remains for burial. She relied on her assistant Mendel for the things that were more physical. Mendel was a large, oafish, mentally challenged strong man whom Servia directed to handle the heavy physical requirements of her job.

As they began their journey to cave number seven, no one spoke of foul play. However, because of the testimony of the seven remaining members of Gamgus's team, there were certainly some serious reservations. "Their story is most difficult, if not impossible, to believe," said Servia to Mendel, who was used to being a sounding board for her private reflection.

"I like their story," replied Mendel. "I think of my mummy and the fairy stories at bedtime when I was little." Servia paused and gawked at him in reaction to his statement and dullard smile.

Chapter 12 - What Awaited Them There

When the expedition arrived at the opening of the rear entrance of cave number seven, Juan and Cephas were the first to light their headlamps, along with four other excavators equipped with hand-digging tools. The goal was to be as respectful as possible to the remains of Gamgus. The coroner and her assistant had with them cloth wraps and a stretcher to carry the remains. The path from the exit side of the cave was a bit of a long tangle to the great cathedral illustrated in the sketch Lauren provided.

Lauren had drawn a large cavern with dismal walls and murky water. The sketch was bleak and somewhat depressing. It portrayed the dark walls and the sconces of smoldering flames. It also showed the altar, prior to the entombment of Gamgus, with the murky and odorous water in front of it. However, when they arrived, this was not what they found. "What in the name of reason is this!" Lauren was in a state of shock at what they were now looking at. "This is not what we left behind us only days ago. It is as if we are in a totally different place."

The walls of the great cathedral were no longer dark, bronze-colored, jagged rock. What was before them now was a beautiful cavern of white limestone walls. A thin film of clear water ran over the surface of the rock walls, giving them the appearance of being coated by a clear porcelain glaze with a glistening sparkle. The great sconces were also changed to a white finish, but instead of containing hot coals smoldering with a low red glow, water flowed from them like great bowls in a feature fountain. The great opening once containing the waterfall as a huge curtain was now completely unobstructed. All the water once flowing over it was now left and right diverted along channels tracing the opening. This allowed the water to empty into the pool, running towards the foot of the altar, where it was no longer green, odorous, and lukewarm, as described by Stan. There were no signs of any smell of sulfur. Instead, the sweet smell of mineral-rich, crystal-clear water surrounded them.

"This can't be right," Mark said, staring in amazement at what was now a completely different cathedral. He reached down from the edge of the now all-white sand altar of Myrobah and scooped up some of the water in his hands. The water smelled sweet, and he decided to taste it. "What in the name of glory!" he said, pausing with a startled and amazed expression. Then, slowly closing his eyes, he continued to drink as he was experiencing some of the most satisfying and purest water he had ever tasted.

"How is this even possible?" exclaimed Hassan. Hassan had studied many geological formations, but nothing could explain what was now before him. It was no longer a huge random pile of black pyrite-infested stone where Gamgus's body had been crushed and entombed. Almost all the rock had been removed, and those remaining appeared as if they had been cut by a stone mason. Each stone was cut away on the top, polished and aligned, leaving an oval-shaped perimeter. The perimeter had an opening facing the exit of the cathedral, as if it were meant for a nonexistent gate. The oval was about twenty feet in diameter, and the cut-stone walls were two feet thick and about two feet high. Inside this magnificent stone courtyard was a bed of pure white sand. The sand was so white the headlamp beams lighting it reflected brighter than they had ever appeared before. In the center of the stone courtyard, on top of the sand, was a glittering golden silhouette of a man lying on his back, as if he were sleeping. The white sand with the gold silhouette was breathtaking in its beauty.

Lauren reached for her sketchpad and began to draw in a frenzy of excitement. "This is the most beautiful and unusual thing I have ever seen," she said, mesmerized by the display. The rest of the team and all the others in the room were captivated and speechless.

"What is the meaning of this, Julius?" said Servia. "We brought manpower to remove tons of stone to retrieve Gamgus's body. This is not what we are looking at here. It appears that someone else has taken the time and effort to memorialize his remains. If it wasn't such an impressive site for a burial, I'd say someone is playing a hoax."

"We are as mystified and caught off guard as you are, Servia," Julius replied. "None of us can explain what has happened here. We are at a loss to comprehend how this could be accomplished in such a short period of time."

"My drawing was not a lie!" Lauren indignantly added. "We all know what we witnessed, and our eyes were not lying to us." With agitated haste, she thumbed through her sketchbook. She found the original drawing and held it open, pointing it towards Juan. "Is this what you saw?"

Juan was at first hesitant to answer, but after a pause he reluctantly nodded his head and replied, "Yes."

"Mark, Julius, Hassan, Stan, and Cephus, how about it?" Lauren asked as she panned the drawing in front of them. The others slowly nodded their heads in agreement. Turning to Servia, Lauren said, "I have an absolute majority agreeing that this drawing accurately represents what was in this spot. None of us can offer a reason why this would not be true. We all swear to it."

"Then, based on what I am seeing right now, this will need to be addressed in a hearing before the House of Magistrates to decide the facts," Servia concluded. "We need to examine the site and bring back as much evidence as we can to present before the House of Magistrates. Hopefully, at the very least, we will find a body."

Then Julius, Servia, and Mendel cautiously entered through the opening of the stone perimeter, careful not to disturb anything. They approached the golden silhouette to get a closer look at it. Julius thought to himself how amazing and odd it was, because it seemed like the pyrite had separated from the black stone to create such a thing. It was impossible for him to conclude that the shape of this silhouette wasn't the work of an artist. It was also very strange, if not impossible, that there wasn't any sign of the particles of black rock present in the pyrite. It sparkled beautifully against the white sand as the light from their headlamps lit the area. Truly none of this could have happened by random occurrence. When they got close enough to really see the silhouette, Julius gasped. What was assumed by all on the outside to be pyrite was not actually pyrite at all. It was, to Julius's amazement, real gold! Not only was it pure gold, but in Julius's expert opinion, it was perhaps the purest he had ever seen. The small particles of gold forming the silhouette appeared to him to be jewelers' quality. Each grain-sized nugget was as if it were fired and polished, ready to receive a mounted gemstone.

"If by any remote chance this is a memorial site done by some other stranger, then I authorize the expedition crew to dig here so we can exhume Gamgus's body," ordered Servia.

"The gold is very pretty; can we take it?" Mendel asked in his low voice.

"Mendel does have a point," replied Julius. "We should do our best to carefully remove all of it before we dig."

Servia gave Mendel a reluctant look and said, "Very good idea, Mendel. You are right to say so." Mendel, not being used to receiving a real compliment from Servia, especially in front of such an important group, gave her a childish smile of accomplishment.

Servia directed the excavation crew to carefully skim the gold silhouette, taking much care to leave none of the gold behind. They had brought with them fifty-pound-capacity cloth bags and were able to fill two of them with the mixture of pure white sand and gold. Because of the quality and varied particle size of gold mixed in the sand, it was unknown how they would separate the two without causing the gold to become less pure than it was. But because the decision needed to be made, and they were limited in resources; they did the best they could in collecting it.

Lauren, in her sketchbook, was drawing what she titled "The Memorial to Gamgus." In her drawing, she captured the perimeter wall and the shape of the silhouette centered inside of it. It was agreed upon that it would be up to the House of Magistrates to decide what to do with the sand and gold.

Once all the gold mixed with sand was carefully retrieved, Servia directed two of the excavators to dig in the spot until they reached Gamgus's body, which they assumed to be buried below. She directed the rest of the crew to explore to the front of the cave, beyond the great cathedral.

"You will need these," Hassan said, handing over his map coordinates that Gamgus had instructed him to make. "Please be careful with them; these are the only copies that exist."

The excavator named Seth gave him an annoyed look, as if Hassan didn't need to tell him what should be obvious. "Hopefully these will prove more reliable than the information that put us on this wild goose chase. I hope, for your sake, a body is found," Seth replied.

Hassan was not a man who took lightly anyone questioning the integrity of his work. "Don't worry, Seth. If you can remember your childhood region scout training, you should have no trouble finding your way around the cave using my coordinates."

"Enough of the pride squabble," interrupted Servia. "You have your orders, Seth. Now get to it." Seth turned reluctantly towards his partner, giving him the signal to get moving. They both stepped into the water and trolled towards the great opening of the falls and soon vanished into the darkness of the other side.

"I sometimes wonder why the council gives me such obstinate, thick-headed help." Mendel gave Servia a sad look, as if he was included in her disappointment. Servia, noticing his countenance, assured him, "Don't worry, my friend. My comments were not meant for you. You have always been cooperative and helpful when I need you." Mendel gave her an endearing look of gratitude. Servia was an important member of the council, but for Mendel's sake she was patient and softhearted with him. Mendel made up for his very low level of intellect with his unwavering devotion and muscle strength, which served her very well.

As the excavators reached about four feet below the surface, Juan commented to Lauren, "I don't think he is here."

"Why would you think that, Juan?" Lauren replied.

Mark interjected, "This whole adventure has been filled with the unexpected. If Gamgus has anything to do with it, things will not be as one would logically conclude."

"After all," Stan added, "his name does mean *not what it appears*, or something like that." For a moment, the seriousness of the situation was met by low laughter from the seven.

But the humor was soon lost when the excavators were nearly far enough down for the walls to be over their heads. Soon a rope would be needed to retrieve them, and the risk of a collapse was becoming imminent.

"Enough!" proclaimed Servia. "We have wasted enough of my time. If there is a body, it certainly isn't here." Turning towards the seven members of Gamgus's team, she expressed her contempt for what was now developing. "I don't know where to begin, but I am starting to believe there is something really nefarious going on."

"I assure you, Servia, we had no intention of wasting valuable resources and are just as put off as you are," said Julius.

"This may be so, Julius, but let me inform you that things are not looking good for you and the others on the team. So far, everything that you said *was* the case is *not* the case. We have a missing person, dead or alive, and you and the rest of your team were all witnesses of Gamgus's last whereabouts. This makes all of you liable and accountable. I have no choice but to end this and return to let the House of Magistrates determine your team's fate."

"Will you at least leave a small team of excavators behind to continue to explore and see if they can find anything more regarding Gamgus and his whereabouts?" asked Mark.

"That is reasonable despite how this is shaping up. But we will need at least one of them to help us carry back the sand and gold." Servia looked down at the two excavators and instructed them to stop digging. After they were lifted out of the empty hole by Cephus and Hassan, she advised one of them to wait for the others and give them instructions. She told him to give them one more day to explore and see if anything else turns up. After that, they would need to immediately return and report their findings. Mendel and the remaining excavator used the stretcher intended for Gamgus's body to carry the heavy bags of sand and gold back to town.

Then Servia, Mendel, the last expedition worker, and the Seven, as they were now being called, began their return to the headquarters of the Council of Magistrates. The Seven were asked many questions by the one expedition worker on the journey back. Questions such as, "Was there ever really a body? Why was the cavern not at all as you described? Where were all the mysterious, terrifying, talking creatures? Are you lying about Gamgus's death, and did he put you up to this? Is this some kind of insidious deception for some unknown gain?" They were all reluctant to give the excavator and the others any more info than what had already been disclosed. The Seven were now being viewed with extreme suspicion, some believing they were concealing something insidious. The team was destined to face the High Council of the House of Magistrates to give account. If it were to be discovered that this was some sort of malicious prank or cover-up, they would be facing a very unpleasant reprimand. They were in the crosshairs of the expedition crew and Servia. She was furious about being brought out for what looked like a charade and a complete waste of her time. Servia had nobody to evaluate, only canvas bags filled with the mystery of pure white sand and gold. But none were more puzzled and disillusioned than the Seven who had witnessed everything. As they walked behind the coroner, her assistant, and the remaining member of the excavation team, they pondered their fate quietly among themselves.

"I can't believe how badly things are going for us," Juan said to Mark in a quiet voice.

"I can't get those damn words Myrobah spoke out of my head," Mark replied. "He said, '*You will live but will surely come to know the worst in me for it.*'"

"I'm beginning to see what he means by that," said Stan, adding to the conversation. "It's clear to me that our fate will fall into the hands of misinformed justice. I can't think of any punishment worse than being locked away or hung for treason, knowing what we know and no one believing us."

"It's obvious Myrobah hid all of the evidence of what he has done, and now he is silencing the only people on the planet who know the truth," added Julius.

"I do find it very odd the way that Myrobah covered his tracks, for lack of a better way to put it. It seems so out of his character to leave such a beautiful and pristine scene. Judging from his prior taste in decorating, I didn't think he had it in him," said Stan.

Cephas and Julius both discreetly broke out into a moment of laughter.

Lauren was in earshot of the exchange and took offense. "I am not finding any humor in any of this. Such irreverent jackasses!" she sternly reprimanded Stan, Cephus, and Julius. The rest of the expedition was unaware of Stan stumbling into a comedic moment and the reaction from Lauren. She was not in the frame of mind to appreciate it. "Let's not forget we lost our friend!" At these words Lauren began to cry again, as the horrid events began to play once more in her head.

Juan, who had caught the end of the interaction, rushed to Lauren and put his arm around her, attempting to console her. "I think you three need to apologize to Lauren," he said with annoyance.

Realizing the gravity of the moment and feeling foolish, Cephas, Stan, and Julius took turns apologizing to Lauren. They all five continued walking together behind the others for a while, with Juan at Lauren's side until she found enough peace to stop crying.

The Seven all agreed they should completely cooperate with the others in the expedition as they were heading back to town. They knew that they needed to give the full account of what they had witnessed, despite the outcome. Once again, for some odd reason, they all believed it was what Gamgus would have wanted them to do.

Chapter 13 - Hearing Before the House of Magistrates

At this point, the human sage named Pondurious paused to read the mood of the townspeople gathered in the courtyard of the gazebo. It was now early afternoon, and the gathering had been sitting and listening for quite a while. The recital was long, and he knew from past experiences that interest and attention could be waning.

Then the young man named Darius piped up, breaking the silent pause, "Pondurious, I think I speak for the rest of us when I say we are all very curious about how it went for the Seven."

"Yes, Pondurious," said the mayor, Fredrick. "Please tell us."

I was also curious about what was going to happen next. The story especially fascinated my interest when it spoke of the water in the cave being once foul and then being found fresh. Allow me now to conclude the story that the sage shared with the gathering of humans.

When they arrived back from the expedition, the Ministry of Excavation supervisor, Alexander, was furious. "What do you mean there were no heavy rocks to be removed? I sent four of my best men equipped with tools to excavate a body from under a collapse."

"Yes, Alexander, and on top of that, there was nobody to be found," added the coroner.

"What a waste of resources. To think I had other commitments that had to be put off for this so-called *emergency mission*. Being told one thing and then finding something else is inexcusable," said Alexander, who was quite incensed. "Nothing came close to resembling what was disclosed for my crew to excavate, and to say the least, it all appears to be a huge sham. Furthermore, having to leave some of my resources behind on a wild goose chase is infuriating!"

"Yes, I certainly agree with you," replied Servia. "The Treasury of the Regions will most certainly appreciate a handsome find of gold, but as for our ministry, a *so-called body* is unacceptable." This was her attempt at sarcasm, letting everyone know her feelings on the Seven. "What was the meaning of being commissioned to retrieve the body of Gamgus, who, I might add, is a highly appreciated asset to the Council of Magistrates, only to return with bags full of pure gold and sand instead. One could conclude Gamgus orchestrated some bizarre act of fraud. Sadly, it appears his weak-minded followers went along with it or, giving them the benefit of the doubt, suffer from a mental illness."

"Are you saying we are weak-minded, mentally disturbed liars attempting to cover our shortcomings, Servia?" retorted Julius, who was not having any of this. "Again, I ask—what did it gain *any* of us to tell a story that contradicted what we found when we returned? You are not using logic."

"Nevertheless, Julius, the facts have presented themselves, and I rest my case. It is now up to the Ministry of Judicial Oversight to sort this out. My citing of the facts against yours will be considered. However, I would say the burden of greatest concern falls on you and your team's shoulders."

Regrettably, Julius thought to himself, *Servia is right*.

Both Alexander and Servia appealed to the House Magistrate of the east group of the Northern Primus Mountains region to arrange and hold a hearing for the Seven. The Seven could not dispute the accusations of the coroner and the supervisor of the expedition because what they held in account and saw confirmed their testimony. But the Seven couldn't deny what they saw prior to when they left the cave the first time either. They were now feeling the walls close in on themselves. They knew by their very testimony they would be condemned, which only added to the grief and anxiety they were already experiencing. But the firsthand witness and accounting of the coroner and supervisor gave ample cause for the decision to hold the hearing. The hearing would decide the team's fate and the course of action to get to the bottom of what had happened to Gamgus, who was still unaccounted for.

The hearing was held at the Town Common Hall, which was open to the public. The word was out about the "Scandal of the Seven," and it drew quite a large crowd. Many had heard of the testimony of Myrobah, the great cave olm. Some others heard about the mythical creatures called mynerts. But most knew of the rumor that Gamgus was destroyed violently and entombed by an avalanche of fallen rock. Not finding the body was the most interesting twist to the Seven's account. All were fascinated by the facts the Seven proclaimed and were very interested in seeing how it would reconcile against the contradictory facts of the expedition team.

The municipal building was a multiuse structure in the town, dedicated for public and private use. It was often a place for celebrations, funerals, and public hearings. It had large, dark oak, arched double doors at the back and a rustic matching platform in the front. The rear double doors served as the main entrance for the public and special guests. The hall had rustic bench seats for the people and a table where Gamgus's team sat facing the stage in front of the hearing table. The platform hosted a long table where the House Magistrate for the east group of the Northern Primus Mountains—the Honorable Helen Winwhisper—and the three council members of the Ministry of Judicial Oversight sat.

The House Magistrate Helen Winwhisper was one of six magistrates that represented each of the three regions and their subregions.

The three members of the Ministry of Judicial Oversight present at the hearing were Carlton Goodall, Alberton Hearding, and Naomi Worthington. Each of the council members was handpicked by the Magistrates of the Primus Regions and could rise to the position of Region Magistrate if they decided to run for the position.

Servia, who represented the Ministry of Health and Sanitation under the Council of Magistrates, and Alexander, who represented the Ministry of Excavation under the same, were also seated at the head table. They would be granted permission to ask any of the Seven questions.

Mark was beginning to wonder how this could be happening and tried to recall the events in his mind. He remembered how he felt when the food in his backpack did not empty during the time in the cave. He remembered their headlamps never needing to be refueled during the entire time, never lacking light. He remembered the voice from the great waterfall everyone on the team heard. He remembered what the great waterfall said and the awful voices of the mynerts. He could never forget the thunderous voice of the great, hideous olm. He remembered Gamgus had spoken strange words when they shared their last meal together and this was when the rations began to diminish. He remembered seeing the vicious bites of the mynerts as they tore Gamgus's flesh from his body, leaving only a bloody, unrecognizable, but still living person. But most of all, he remembered the hideous laughter of the great olm and the terrifying shrieks of the hundreds of mynerts echoing behind them as they were forced to leave. All of it was now a nightmarish memory he would never forget. This, along with the sketches and recorded writings of the events were to be shared with the special committee hearing before the Ministry of Judicial Oversight.

"All rise," announced Head Councilman Alberton as he banged his gavel. Everyone in the room stood silent in their places. "The Honorable Magistrate of the East Primus

Mountains region, Helen Winwhisper, presiding over this hearing, will now introduce this case before us."

"Thank you, Councilman," she replied. "This hearing is to determine the course of action to be taken to settle the discrepancies between the cave number seven GLMO team and the Council of Magistrates. Now, please be seated." Everyone in the room took their seats. "What we are here today to deliberate and determine are all the events leading up to the disappearance of Gamgus and whether there was any malice of persons or misappropriation of the Magistrates' resources." She then turned her attention

to the coroner. "Coroner Servia, could you please give us your account of what you witnessed, and feel free to ask any questions of the defendants before you."

Servia opened with, "Thank you, Your Honor. As you may be aware, my expertise was called upon to accompany a retrieval mission upon request of the returning expedition team surveying cave number seven on the east side of the Calvert Mountains. I regret to inform you that we were commissioned under false pretenses. What was described by the remaining members of Gamgus's expedition team was not at all what we found." She then directed her first question to Julius. "Julius, you told us that there was a collapse of rock crushing Gamgus and entombing him under it. When we got to the location, we found no pile of the black stone you described. What we did find was a strange stone perimeter encompassing a bed of pure, sun-bleached sand containing the shape of a man's silhouette made of fine, granular gold. Giving the benefit of the doubt to your recollection, we decided to excavate the so-marked area to find a body. We found nothing. No evidence of an avalanche of stone, no evidence of blood, and no remains of a body. How do you explain all of this?"

An unexpected noise was heard just then, coming from the chamber area in the hall, breaking the silence following her question.

"What is the meaning of this interruption, Treasury Minister Marcus?" said the Head Magistrate.

The Minister of the Treasury, who had just entered the room, stopped in front of her and answered, "Your Honor, I wanted to report to members of this hearing the results of our evaluation of the sand and gold mixture presented for analysis."

"Do you think it will add to validate the stories presented at this hearing?" replied Councilman Alexander.

"I wouldn't have bothered to interrupt these proceedings if I hadn't felt it necessary to disclose the most unusual and incredible findings. This will certainly offer more to consider," answered Marcus.

"Yes, Marcus," interjected Magistrate Winwhisper. "Please inform us."

"The experts in the Ministry of the Treasury cannot explain the quality and the condition of the gold mixed in the sand. It's as if the gold had been processed by a very advanced and pure-firing kiln. The surfaces of even the smallest particles had a mirror finish and contained no traces of impurity. Such a finding begs the question…why would anyone leave such a treasure behind?" Marcus explained.

"That is most strange, Marcus. Like much of what has been different in the two versions of what had happened in cave number seven," replied Alexander, now appearing annoyed by the revelation. No one in the Town Common Hall could give any explanation for something which had never been accomplished and why it would have been abandoned for anyone to discover.

"Julius," Servia continued, "despite this newly discovered fact, you were asked a question."

"Could you repeat the question, Servia?" replied Julius.

Servia impatiently rephrased it, "How do you explain the discrepancy of your facts against ours?"

"All that has been revealed to the expedition team, and to us seven, appears to defy logic, so I can only speculate on what appears illogical," answered Julius.

"So, you mean another lie?" Servia snorted.

"I did not say the word *lie*, Coroner, I said *speculate on what appears illogical*. What I know to be true appears to defy what is logical. It appears to me that what we witnessed must have been removed and what was found is a mystery to solve and certainly not criminal. It is only illogical because the time span to accomplish what was found by the expedition and what my team and I witnessed prior should be next to impossible to accomplish. It would have required a coordinated effort that demonstrates powers beyond any known capability," replied Julius.

"So, for all intents and purposes, Julius, you and your team are part of a well-coordinated lie?" sneered Servia.

"This is an intolerable and impossible situation!" barked out Mark. "There were many unexplainable and so-called *impossible* things that happened. How do you explain that we had headlamp fuel and food rations for only a day and a half and yet we ate and had constant light for over three days?"

"So, you say," piped up Alexander.

"So, *all of us* say!" Lauren, who was now beginning to boil with frustration, snapped at Alexander. "Next, you are going to say all my drawings are just fiction!"

Realizing what Lauren had just said, Alexander replied, "Exactly, drawings of fiction. Your Honor, I would like to offer to the council that Gamgus's team members offer proof that they were at the very least derelict in their duties. We do not pay for drawings that belong in a storybook of fables for children. Are you telling me that a *mynert,* which you drew so well, *isn't* a fictitious beast that belongs in a fairy tale?"

Lauren was now remembering the horrible sight of her dear friend being ripped to bloody shreds before her eyes. This was a sight that she could never unsee, and she replied with anger, tears beginning to well in her eyes, "You insensitive, condescending bastard. If you had only been there!"

"Order in this hearing!" the presiding Magistrate Winwhisper said as she rapped her gavel to quell the noise that was erupting from the crowd in the hall. "May I remind the seven accused before us that it is for the very reason your account contradicts the excavation crew and the coroner's that we are here. Up to this point in this hearing, you have failed to give us any reason or proof to believe your account. Unless you can bring to us any new evidence that can give us reason to believe yours over ours, this hearing will now need to recess to deliberate a course of action. Julius, is there anything you or the others in your team would like to offer in your defense, or the whereabouts of Gamgus, alive or dead?"

"I would like to point out a couple of things," Hassan spoke, in reply to the final request.

"Yes, Hassan, you may proceed," said Magistrate Winwhisper.

"While it is true that our cartographer is a very talented artist, she is also an expert in her field. The council is aware of my qualifications and knows that I rely on an accurate assessment of structures to facilitate my work. While it is true that the area of the cave that is in question appeared to be different than what was described, I assure you that structurally it is identical. Only the veneer was found different. Lauren's drawing does capture the details needed to prove this to be true. She captured the sconces, the opening area of the falls and the altar we described to the council. We are only arguing over the details, not the actuals."

"Pretty substantial details, wouldn't you say?" interjected Councilman Hearding.

Then Stan added, "And of course, the water in Lauren's drawing I described as green and odorous, while what was found was clear and of the purest quality. The common fact is that Lauren's drawing showed the water formation and location as we both found it."

"Minor discrepancies, Stan?" Councilwoman Worthington announced with an incensed tone in her voice.

"And even if the huge rock pile was found to be a cut-stone garden perimeter, the stone was pyrite-infested black stone," added Julius. "I think if you do a before and after overlay of the footprint of both, you will find them to be the same relative size.

"Let us not lose sight of the most significant reason for this hearing, ladies and gentlemen," Head Councilman Goodall's voice cut through the comments. "I think I speak for this committee that the Seven are trying to cast reasonable doubt in the hopes that we cannot conclude foul play. This is understandable since they are aware that they face serious repercussions for what appears evident to this council. But let us not forget what I believe is of paramount concern to this hearing: Gamgus is missing or dead. Unfortunately for the remaining team, these so-called *details*, despite some extraordinary mysteries, are all we have for reaching a conclusion. The only question I have is why they chose such a bad strategy to cover what appears to be foul play. Certainly, they could have constructed a story that would not have allowed such discrepancies."

Then Juan spoke, "Perhaps that would be the strongest argument for the truth. Why would we have made up a story so far from the details of the facts? What about the sand and gold? Certainly, if it was foul play, it would have been hidden so it could be recovered when we returned covertly to steal it from the House of Magistrates."

Now the room was silent. It was a conundrum of statements and questions, which caused a pause in the hearing. Then the crowd began to break the silence as a low rumble of debate erupted. The noise was quickly extinguished by the rapping crescendo of Magistrate Winwhisper's gavel. "Council members, defendants, ladies and gentlemen in this hall. If there is nothing else to add, I would like to make a motion for the council of this hearing to take recess to deliberate what would be a just course of action. Are there any objections?" The room was once again silent. "Do I have a motion to recess for the purpose of deliberation?"

Councilman Hearding replied, "I motion we recess to discuss as Magistrate Winwhisper recommends."

"Do we have a second?" added Magistrate Winwhisper.

"I second," said Servia.

"Motion approved." Magistrate Winwhisper slammed her gavel. The council and the magistrate rose and walked into the chamber room to deliberate the course of action. The Seven sat silent and still while the rest of the room began to murmur and discuss among themselves, awaiting the return of the magistrate and the council members.

When the committee for the hearing returned and all were seated, Magistrate Winwhisper shared the decision of the council. "Gamgus was a man of inapproachable wisdom, knowledge, and action. He, in all the years we have known him, never failed to offer valuable and insightful solutions to any challenge given to him. He was well-known and liked by his peers and loved by his closest friends. To say he is or will be missed is an understatement. The remaining members of his team have always proved loyal and worked very well with him. They are considered our best team at what they do and, up to this point have remained loyal, trustworthy, and indispensable." There was a low applause acknowledging the truth of her statement. Many knew of Gamgus and his team's reputation and were not shy to agree with the magistrate. "However," she continued, "we cannot accept the story they have told to us today." The crowd grew tense and some were murmuring to each other. "The council has decided there is some form of deception, or worse yet, malfeasance, which has been perpetrated. It is the council's conclusion that the team either has conspired against the Magistrates of the Primus Regions for reasons unknown, or they are suffering from a mental delusion because of a mind-altering agent encountered while in the cave. Logic dictates it cannot be the latter because it would be impossible for all accounts to be as identical as they are. The critical fact is that Gamgus is missing and not able to give an account. This places his team in an unfortunate position. The council cannot rule out the possibility that Gamgus conspired with them, but until he appears or is found, the council has decided on a course of action. By the authority given to me and this council by the Magistrates of the Primus Regions, it has been decided the team before us has been relieved of all duties and responsibilities. All permissions to perform future services have been suspended. They will be required to serve confinement for no less than a year in order to be evaluated. The term of confinement will continue until a satisfactory resolution is obtained by evidence and facts presented through continued discovery. If such information is revealed, then further action will be decided by hearing or trial."

Those who were guests in the hall and those who were friends and family of the Seven began to erupt in arguing protest. The noise in the room began to swell while those for Gamgus and his team argued with those on the side of the council. Minister Winwhisper began to bang her gavel louder and louder, shouting, "Order in the hall, order!" But the arguing escalated to the point where it was beginning to turn physical. The hearing was spinning out of control until a light knocking at the rear doors of the hall caused a dead silence to fall over the room. One might question how such a meek knock could penetrate the ears of everyone in the room and startle them to silence. All eyes were now turned and fixed on the doors as security for the Magistrates slowly opened them. The crowd gasped at what they saw.

Entering the room was a man dressed in a white robe. The robe was like a garment used by clergy during a wedding ceremony. It was ornate and pristine, without a blemish. The fringes were embroidered with silver and gold patterns of shapes and symbols which were mysterious and unfamiliar. His sandals were burnished leather straps being held together by polished small silver buckles. His skin was dark, like he had spent many hours and days in the sunlight. There was a very unusual property to his skin. At first glance it appeared he was covered with pockmarks, but as he walked closer to the stage and through the assembly, the marks were seen to have a golden sparkle, and it became apparent that they were embedded golden stones. It was as if he stood in front of a great blast and the particles of stone were shot into his flesh. They appeared to be old wounds which were now healed, the marks of an event in the past and worn as a reminder of it.

It was Lauren who first noticed and shouted out, "Gamgus!" She broke the ranks of the inquiry and ran towards him, throwing her arms around him, kissing his cheeks while tears of joy began to fall from her eyes. Mark, Julius, Stan, Hassan, Cephas, and Juan stood in stunned silence. When they realized who was standing in front of them, they also broke into a run and descended on Gamgus with tears and rejoicing. Then Lauren said through her tears, "We left you for dead; how is this possible?!" The others stood back with amazed and dumbfounded expressions. Julius couldn't help but notice the small glittering marks on the skin of Gamgus were small particles of pyrite. While all this was taking place, the hall erupted into a frenzy of murmuring and stares. Fingers were pointing while the council for the hearing all stood with contemptible expressions, conferring with each other.

"Order, Order! Order in the hall!" shouted Magistrate Winwhisper as she was violently banging her gavel. Slowly, everyone took their seats.

Gamgus and his team were now facing the front where Magistrate Winwhisper, the council members, the coroner, and Head of Excavation stood, glaring at them. "What is the meaning of this, Gamgus?" Head Councilman Goodall gruffly barked. "Please explain yourself!"

Then Gamgus answered with a question for the councilman, "What did my team, who were firsthand witnesses, testify to in this hearing?"

Councilman Goodall replied, "A most impossible story, and obviously a lie since now we see you are not dead. In fact, you appear to be quite well, better than well even. I would say you have been off on an unauthorized holiday and have come back with the spoils of your frolic." The crowd erupted into low laughter and the Head Councilman appeared to be quite pleased with his own wit and clever observation.

Then Gamgus asked the Head Councilman this question: "Sir, how can you conclude my team is lying since you were not there to see what they saw?"

The Head Councilman seemed not to be impressed with Gamgus and replied in a snide tone, "Then perhaps, Gamgus, you could tell your side of the story, and we will see if it collaborates with your team's." The Head Councilman now had an expression of satisfaction on his face, as if he had trapped Gamgus and was anticipating a rich and unbelievable story.

Gamgus approached the front of the council, facing them. After a pause, he slowly turned to face his beloved seven. He smiled affectionately at them. Then he turned to face the crowd who were present at the hearing, addressing everyone in the room. "Honorable Magistrate Winwhisper, council members," glancing at the Seven, "friends," then facing the assembled in the hall, "family and all others concerned." He then took a measured pause and continued, "Until just recently, all my Father had made had been separated from the perpetual, as He knew would happen, because it *had* to happen. This reality was an existence cut off from what sustains it. It has been like a mighty river which supplies its water to a city. It being the only source of water, life ends in the city when a great dam is built to prevent the water from reaching it. Unless the water is allowed to flow by opening its gates, all life begins to die. While all is dying, water stores are depleted, and all that exists and is left will eventually evaporate and dilute until none can be found. Divide and conquer is established and becomes the new law of the land. So it has been in this world we live in. But do not lose heart. All which was cut off when I and my team entered the cave at the foothills of the Calvert Mountains is being restored to the source of life."

"What is he saying?" Mark quietly asked Julius, who looked back puzzled, shrugging his shoulders. The Great Hall remained silent. Gamgus was disclosing something much larger than the accusations of an elaborate hoax.

Gamgus continued, "In our existence of reality, there are turning points. They define and determine the course of the universe, shaping the physical and spiritual world we live in. My team and I are witnesses and participants of what will continue as a new point on the timeline of universal history. It will move us forward into a new age of a powerful absolute reality in which all living in it will be forever changed. Just as time passing demonstrated death and decay, time moving forward will now prove new life and growth instead. It will be, as an old parable once said, about a tree which had died and was cut down. As if defying physical law, new shoots began to sprout from the dead stump. One day it will become a new tree, with a renewed nature, stronger, more vibrant, and changed forever. This new reality will make its way known to the far reaches of the universe and to the deepest depths of all life and matter."

"This sounds like madness, Gamgus, how could any of what you are saying even be possible?" snapped Head Councilman Goodall in reply, clearly disturbed and agitated.

Gamgus replied, addressing the room, "Because humanity was the crowning achievement of the work of my Father, humanity would be the highest factor in directing the course of all my Father had made. Humanity was fashioned in the image of the *Why*, who is my Father, and so all it represents must reflect the true nature of Who made it. It was necessary that humanity should turn its back on Who made it. Only then could it find itself in longing, desiring a wondrous homecoming. The enemies of my Father, who also came into existence by His will and design but not as a portrayal of Himself, were not made capable of receiving mercy. This is because, by their created purpose, they were void of this ability. This was at the core of their jealousy and enmity towards the *Why*, *Reason* and the *Mission*. This was by my Father's design and for His good purpose; it had to be so. They are sealed by the mission of their purpose and not with the desire of a free will to fulfill the miracle of faith. These were many of the embodied creatures we met in the caves of the Calvert Mountains who sought, through their blindness, to destroy the *Reason* and the *Mission* of the *Why*. All my team has reported is true. The *Mission* in my Father was inspired and fulfilled by the lower purpose that the Council of Magistrates commissioned my team and I to perform."

The room erupted into a clamor of disturbed conversation. Magistrate Winwhisper began slamming her gavel while shouting, "Enough, enough! You are out of order, Gamgus! The story your team told us described unbelievable events.

No one has ever witnessed anything the likes of the creatures your team described. They claim they witnessed your death by a torture no human could endure. The very fact you are standing here before us is proof you are lying before this hearing. The very fact you concur with their story places you at the center of this deception. And now you dare claim to have a higher calling than the Magistrates, which hold the power to sentence you and your team for contempt and treason!"

Gamgus then announced to the council, "You have no authority beyond what was given to you by my Father."

At these words, the House Magistrate erupted, banging her gavel and angrily pronouncing, "How dare you speak such words of defiance and high treason! You are mad and should face the highest punishment offered in this land! I hold you in contempt of this hearing!" Then calling on the Ministers of Security, she commanded, "Place this man under arrest!" The crowd in the hearing room swelled to its highest point of clamor.

Gamgus, in defiance, turned his back on the council to address his seven loyal friends and the crowd, shouting over the noise. "My dearest friends and all in this chamber. It is with great joy and purpose I now say these final words to all who will listen and receive them!" At this proclamation, the crowd drew silent. Strangely, the Head Magistrate and the council were all now fixed on Gamgus. Each of the Seven exchanged silent and troubled glances at the words Gamgus just spoke and the effect it had on the gathering.

"What do you mean by *final* words, Gamgus?" said Servia, breaking the silence.

Gamgus answered her while facing all in the room. "My Father sent me to break the spell enslaving your existence from the beginning of time, because humanity believed the lie. Because I am sent by Him, through the miracle of being born human, having all humanity possesses but not under the sentence of the highest treason, I am the only free human. This means only I could offer myself to the ruler of the fallen as a ransom for your freedom. Only a perfect sacrifice could satisfy the cause and effect of a severed relationship, which would exist forever alone, enslaved to self. I am this sacrifice who willingly laid down on the altar of Myrobah to receive all the disbursement due by the law of entropy. But because the *Why*, *Reason*, and *Mission* have always been and will always be, I could not remain in complete atrophy. The very will of the *Why* and His perpetual nature could not be contained by the prison of His enemies. Nor could it be contained by the natural cause and effect of a law meant for future grace. The passion and affection existing in the *Why* raised the *Reason* through the *Mission*. Because it always would be that I would be given new life, I demonstrate this same passion and affection to all humanity. This has been given freely for all who will trust and desire the *Reason* by the *Mission* in the *Why*. This trust and desire can only come if you believe and trust what has been freely given to you."

"How are we going to do this?" said Julius to Gamgus. "I think I speak for the rest of the team in saying that we are broken and at the end of ourselves."

"You, my friend, are right where you need to be," assured Gamgus. "I now leave you with the *Mission,* who walks with me. You too will receive Him and carry Him ever before you. The *Mission* will live in you, guiding you to the final day where all will be reconciled to the perpetual realm of my Father. You will know the gratitude and joy coming from co-laboring in this great work and experience my presence and help alongside you. This work offers the opportunity to hear and receive the amazing news of restoration to the perpetual. Those hearts who truly believe will forever desire and trust in the *Why, Reason,* and *Mission.*"

And it was with these words that Gamgus stretched out his hands as if awaiting the embrace of the room. Then a radiant light began to glow from within him. As the light caused those in the room to shield their eyes, he proclaimed these parting words, "And now I leave to return to my place in the *Why* and *Mission*. The *Mission* I now leave with you in my place until I return on the day of fulfillment. Do not lose heart, for in the *Mission* I will always be with you until the end of the age."

And it was with those final words that the light emanating from Gamgus became as bright as the sun, making it impossible to see him. He was now becoming a great orb of light, slowly rising to the ceiling, lighting the Great Hall. Outside, the sky was full of the faithful stewards of the *Why, Reason,* and *Mission*. They looked like giant, sunlit humanoids in white robes, with glowing golden currents of wind swirling around their bodies. They were majestically suspended in the air by the wondrous air currents while they were singing beautiful choruses of music no one could understand. This music filled the land, echoing like a giant tubed wind chime thunderously belling. The wondrous resonating tones could be heard from inside and outside and far away, causing all who were outside to look into the sky. The growing intensity of the orb of energy and light was becoming as bright as a star. After rising to the ceiling of the Great Hall, it passed through the roof as if it had no mass nor was made of any matter. All in the gathering broke ranks and began to pour out the exit of the Great Hall.

"You have not been dismissed!" yelled Magistrate Winwhisper, who was now banging her gavel with a frustrated fury. As the great orb of light and energy rose up in the sky towards the realm of the constellations, it swelled in size until it occupied the skies with the gathering of the faithful stewards who were singing the mysterious song of adoration and accolades.

As the magnificent sight unfolded, the hall was emptied and all who attended had spilled out into the great courtyard outside, looking up at the awesome scene unfolding in the skies above them. Then the whole display—Gamgus as the magnificent star and all of the faithful stewards—slowly moved up and into the canopy of the sky. Together they became a small sun, growing smaller and smaller until there wasn't enough light to even be seen anymore. Many others saw the event from afar, but only those in the hall knew what had happened and what it meant. All others would have to be told by those who had witnessed the origins of the event.

Chapter 14 - The Book and the Amulet

The human sage named Pondurious spoke the last words of his incredible account. It was now approaching late afternoon and the human gathering before me had been sitting and listening for a long time. He looked back and forth at the townspeople, anticipating a response from them. There was a long, reflective silence as the crowd slowly swayed in their seats, finding no words to say about the unfolding of events told. It was a lot to take in. I was also at a loss about what to conclude and was left without anything inside me except the poisoned yet longing essence of my water.

Then the researcher and developer, Rorke, broke the silence. "Well, well, Pondurious. Such a *wonderful* story of folly and fantasy," he said with sarcasm. The crowd broke out into a low rumble of laughter. "Although thought-provoking and entertaining," he said, "what good can possibly come from it? Even if any of it were true, what possible solution could it provide to remedy the current situation?"

"The good is the hope the story brings. The solution has yet to be revealed," answered the sage. The gathering was brought back to a pensive silence.

"Hope is for dreamers and that which isn't grounded in reality!" Rorke barked back, being unnerved by the silence and attention now being directed at him. "Even if there is a great cosmic *Why* behind all matter and order of our existence, what makes you think it, or *whoever*, would even care about a small town's crisis, such as ours?" The crowd surrounding them started murmuring again.

Then the scientist named Argon said with a raised voice, "People, people, hear me out! While I too agree that his story is outlandish and full of fantasy and mythology, I cannot argue the scientific possibility of its construct." Argon had the crowd's attention as the gathering settled down once more, anticipating his comments. "While it is true most of the story has been embellished with mystery and mystical events, I cannot argue the logic at its core. It speaks of the law of entropy and all things racing towards atrophy, or death, if you are too simple to comprehend the scientific term for it. The great, for lack of a better word, *hope* of science is in the physical realm we all live in. The discovery of a means for exact balance would yield to the perpetual. Such a discovery would launch the sciences into a new frontier. A discovery such as this would prove all could be explained. It also would prove the human mind is an evolving phenomenon because of many millions of years of evolution. Order of this kind comes from random energy and matter colliding long enough until patterns are formed. However, the mythology of a great *Why*, the creator of all things, having some petty desire for its creation is unscientific and is unprovable; therefore, it is not valid." Then the scientist directed his gaze at the sage. "Tell me this, Pondurious, can you present scientific proof of your story?"

"To presume all is answered inside the narrow walls of your perception of pure science limits the true nature of what pure science is," answered the sage. Argon's expression shifted from cocky assurance to a startled, insulted bewilderment at this statement. "Is it not a fact that all things must be subject to absolute truth, which cannot be contradicted, otherwise it is not true or absolute?

"Of course, Pondurious. I do believe this to be scientific fact," answered Argon.

"Science, like all things under the sun," continued Pondurious, "must conform to this or could not exist otherwise. Wouldn't you agree, Argon?"

The human scientist Argon, now being caught off guard at the logic, stumbled to reply, "Well, um, of course, Pondurious. This is obvious."

"So," the sage concluded, "pure science can only prove what *is*, it cannot prove what is *not*. If *your* science chooses to discredit what is claimed to be true by proclaiming something is not possible or provable, then it suffers the folly of doing this very thing. Therefore, yours is *not* pure science and you embrace deception."

Argon had no comment, rolling his eyes, and with a belittling and stumped pronouncement, blurted out, "Rubbish!"

Then the young human named Darius, who had asked for the name of the *Why*, *Reason*, and the *Mission*, spoke up and asked, "Sir, where did you come from? Do you know any other sages such as you? I have heard of others, and you are certainly not from around here."

"I come from a line of those who were firsthand witnesses of that hearing held by the Magistrates of the Primus Regions," said the sage. Pondurious had a kind smile on his face. It appeared to me he had taken a liking to the young man. "This account has been handed down from generation to generation and has been told to many in many lands."

"It is an amazing account, sir," Darius said. "But I am concerned that since it is very old, how is it possible it has not lost its original meaning while being passed down?"

"I have sojourned from that land, formally named the Primus Regions, on the specific mission of sharing its story with others. Much of my life has been dedicated to preserving and recalling precisely what I have shared with you today." answered Pondurious.

"This is the same area I mentioned earlier!" Suddenly standing up and interrupting the discourse was the mayor, Fredrick. "A land rich with culture and containing many mysteries from the past. I am once again taken back that all we are discussing today seems to center around it." The mayor looked about at the humans in the gathering, seemingly pleased with himself, before slowly sitting down. His mousey scribe, Ditimus, began to frantically make notes in his book, recording this interruption. Ditimus seemed sure he'd win favor for notating Mayor Fredrick's "vast knowledge" of the planet.

"Yes, you are quite correct, Mayor Fredrick." The sage nodded with a kind smile directed at the mayor. "The hearing on that day was dismissed and all charges were dropped. All involved in the hearing were without excuse and had to accept the story of the Seven as historic truth. But even so, not all chose to believe. But many more were changed forever that day, and the mission of the town became dedicated to telling the story of what had happened, appealing to anyone who would listen and believe it. The Magistrate of the east side of the North Primus Mountains region decided to commission all things recorded by the Seven and the written accounts of the hearing to be preserved and held safe. Dedicated servants were given the task of doing RCS copies of Lauren's maps and drawings. Painstaking proofs were made of all the writings from the Seven and the court recorder for the hearing. The proofs were made into copies and assembled to be contained in books that would be given to those dedicated to telling the historic story."

"So, sir, you are saying that you have written proof from the original sources that confirm the account shared with us today?" said Darius with excitement on his face.

"Yes, young man," assured Pondurious.

"Do you have any of the writings with you?" asked the young man.

Pondurious paused and looked around at the crowd, who were now fixing all their attention on the young man and the sage. Turning his attention back to Darius, "I have one of the books, young man."

"Please, sir, may I see it?" The sound in the young man's voice was of desperate excitement.

"I will show you the book, but you must promise me to be very careful with it since it is very old and valuable."

Then, turning to the mayor, the sage asked Fredrick to announce to the crowd that no harm should become of it and that it is for the young man's eyes only.

The mayor nodded and announced to the crowd, "Pondurious has agreed to show the proof of the historic account to us, but only the son of my friend Felix shall touch it!" Everyone in the crowd, both the skeptic and the hopeful, were all intrigued and silently nodded their heads to agree.

Pondurious reached into his shoulder pack and pulled out a beautifully crafted book bound with animal hide. The book was very old, clearly handed down from father to son for many generations. The pages were made of heavy parchment and filled with a type of print which looked like a very old style of writing. These were real examples of the reactive process used to reproduce the original text and drawings. The images were not perfect, as I have seen in papers the humans would read while relaxing in my courtyard. But it was obvious they came directly from the originals. Then Pondurious, with a smile on his face, carefully handed the book to Darius.

The young man began to carefully thumb through the book, stopping and exclaiming to the crowd as certain titles and items leaped off the pages. "Look!" he said. "This chapter contains the notes from Cephas about the mynerts and the great olm! It also records the dialogue of the waterfall, Gamgus, and the conversations He had with the team!" He continued with even more excitement. "This chapter has the coordinates of the cave recorded by Julius and Stan!" And as his excitement began to increase, his voice became louder. "This chapter is from the log of Mark, which contained records of the provisions the team used, accompanied by his comments and reflections!" But then he became quiet as if he couldn't believe what he was seeing. With a sober and serious tone in his voice, but no less awestruck than before, he said to the crowd, "These pages contain the copies of the drawings done by Lauren, showing everything she captured while in the cave." On the pages before him were the drawings of the swarming mynerts, the beautiful mirrored underground lake, the towering waterfall the voice came from, the dark cathedral of Myrobah, and all the others Lauren had sketched. The young man slowly looked up at Pondurious with wonderment in his expression. He had no words about what he was feeling until great tears of joy began to fall from his face.

Pondurious moved towards the young man to hold and console him until he was able to contain himself. "Why are you crying, young man?" he asked.

"Sir, I now see the reality of what is before me and understand there is a hope and purpose for the present and what lies ahead in the future. This vision has given me such cause as to believe and follow in a new path of hope and light."

"You are one of very few who only needed to hear the story and see the words and works recorded to make such a great profession. Greater will be your joy and hope as more will be revealed to you in the future," proclaimed the sage to the young Darius.

Then Darius looked into the sage's eyes. "How have you come to be so wise and believe such things?"

"I was once young like you, and I see myself in you," answered Pondurious. "I, too, heard the words, saw the pages of this book, and was so moved, as you are now."

Then Darius, wiping the tears from his eyes, noticed the amulet hanging around Pondurious's neck. The amulet was white porcelain set in an antique brass frame that was closed with a sturdy silver clasp. On the porcelain face of the amulet was an artistic cast silhouette of a human figure surrounded by an oval-shaped line, a small section of the line missing at the side of the silhouette. "I think I know what that symbol is in the middle of your amulet," Darius said to the sage.

"That would be a strong possibility. I described it in the account." Then the sage reached for the book the young man was holding and thumbed to one of the pages.

Darius lit up with excitement at what he saw. "My word, sir! This is a picture that Lauren drew of what was found when they returned to cave number seven!" The picture was the strange pyrite rock border that surrounded the gold silhouette of the resting man, which mirrored the symbol on the amulet.

"That is correct, young man," said Pondurious.

"Then, inside the amulet…" Darius came to a sudden stop, as if he was about to ask the impossible. He looked up at Pondurious with anticipation.

"Yes, you are correct, my dear friend." This was the first time the sage referred to the young Darius as a *dear* friend.

"What is in the amulet, Pondurious?" Argon interjected.

"Yes, please tell us," Agreed Rorke.

The sage paused, then smiled. "It was the last thing to touch Gamgus's body after he had died."

"What do you mean by 'the last thing'?" asked the mayor, Fredrick. "Wasn't it the avalanche of stone that was the last thing to touch his body?"

"Don't you see?" Darius cut in with excitement. "It is the sand and the gold found when the expedition crew returned. I can't explain it, but whatever happened to the body of Gamgus, the sand and gold were what remained because of it. I can't explain why I am convinced this is true but, in my heart, I can't deny what screams out."

"Are you saying that one mystery was traded for another, son?" said Darius's father, Felix, who had kept silent until now.

"Yes and no," Pondurious answered on Darius's behalf. "I think your son has had an epiphany." Turning to the young man, he asked him a question. "Am I correct in saying that you believe that a miracle was exchanged for a miracle?"

Darius was now even more excited. "Well yes, sir. I think you have said exactly what I know to be true. The word *miracle* is one rarely used around here. It is mostly said when parents tell mythical stories to their children, or for something impossible that can't be explained."

The sage was endeared towards the young man more than ever. "May I ask what your name is, young man?" The crowd drew in a gasp. It was custom in those days to acknowledge the parents in public, while their sons or daughters remained silent during public discourse. This was out of respect for their parents, and unless called upon by the head of the household, their opinions were typically not heard. However, it was obvious that the father, Felix, had given his son a more prominent status by allowing him to question the sage. This is why, up to this point, Pondurious didn't even know the young man's name.

"My name is Darius," answered the young man.

Pondurious once again smiled at the young man. "Dearest Darius." Now the sage was expressing that the young man had won special favor in his eyes. "In the perpetual realm of Ram, nothing is without possibility. By the very will of the *Why*, the *Mission* is seen by us in the *Reason,* and ALL in the *Reason* is natural. So, in the minds of that which was connected to the perpetual and became severed and subject to the law of entropy, there is what is natural and what is supernatural. This is because the mind that is subject to the law of entropy cannot reason beyond its limits, being subject to death."

"So, are you saying, sir, that the natural and the supernatural are really one and the same?" Darius asked the sage.

"Yes, Darius," the sage answered. "It is only the fact that our existence is lived out under the law of entropy that we cannot comprehend this. But I am here to announce to all who will accept that the door of opportunity has been forever opened to seek and to know Ram through the finished work of the *Reason* who lived with us."

Darius, now even more full of joy, blurted out in excitement, "So it is true that there is some of the *supernatural* white sand and gold inside the amulet!" All at once, the crowd gasped and turned their focus from the young human's excitement and swung their stares to the sage. The crowd was more interested than ever, murmuring among each other as if something exciting was about to happen.

The sage, noticing the crowd in anticipation for a confirmation, replied, "When the excavation team gathered the sands mixed with the refined gold left in place of Gamgus's body, it was kept safeguarded by the House of Magistrates. At first, it was to be examined and analyzed. They were going to sift the sand from the gold and keep the gold safely with the Treasury of the Regions. But after the events of the hearing, most everyone in the town who had witnessed the supernatural departure of Gamgus were changed. They believed they were part of a great turning point in the history of the world and the universe. It was believed Gamgus had left this material behind for a specific purpose. For certain, it was determined to be used to offer support for the truth of the *Mission*."

"What do you mean by 'the truth of the *Mission*,' Pondurious?" said Felix.

Pondurious replied, "As I said before, the nature of Ram the perpetual is in the relationships of the name. The person of the *Why* being in a relationship with the person of the *Reason*, all being one with the person of the *Mission*. Since Gamgus demonstrated on the day of the great hearing, He, being the *Reason* is now with the *Why*. The person of the *Mission* has been left behind to be known by and in us."

"This is a most curious play on words, Pondurious," remarked Rorke. "What in the name of all before us does this have to do with the sand and the gold you claim to hold?"

The sage elaborated, "The sand and gold are the physical evidence of the person of the *Mission* who dwells in the hearts of those who are called to serve Ram. Since there was only a small amount of the material, it was cherished, and only very small quantities could be handled, for the sole purpose of proclaiming the hope for the new world of the perpetual. It would also be referred to as the very proof Ram gave to what was dearest to Him. This would be, as it always was, a means of courting the hearts of humanity to long for and trust in Him. It was decided by the Magistrates of the Primus Regions that all who carry in their purpose as leaders of the *Mission* would hold close to their hearts the very dust and gold that remained when Ram ransomed all by His gift of self-sacrifice. All who share in the hope of the *Mission* and share in the final meal with Gamgus have access to this sand and dust as the *Mission* calls them to use it. It has been proven if one desires and believes Ram is able to do all things, then only a very, very small amount of the sand and gold will perform great works no human could ever hope to accomplish alone, or united as many."

"Sir," said the young Darius, now with the most determined and serious tone he could offer. "May we have a very small amount of this sand and gold? I have no doubt that if we were to add this to the water of our well, the very will of Ram the perpetual would be done."

"Why do you ask this of me, Darius?" the sage asked him.

"Sir, I believe it is Ram's will. I believe He can and will, if He is sought, and that it would only take a few grains of the sand and gold to accomplish the healing of the well's water supply."

What was this young human saying? I thought to myself. A few grains of sand and gold amount to nothing compared to the mass quantities of caustic elements that have entered my underground canals. The scientist named Argon stood up, unknowingly concurring with me when he said, "This is absurd, Felix! I think it is time to tell your son that enough is enough. Why we *ever* let you allow him to speak among us only proves why the gullibility of youth should not be our guide."

"There has *certainly* been more than enough gullibility in your intellectual arrogance, Argon!" Felix snapped back.

"Now, now, gentlemen," Mayor Fredrick interjected in a patronizing tone. "Let us not insult each other. Please sit down, you two." Felix and Argon sat down slowly while they exchanged stern looks with each other. "Pondurious, have you more to add? I believe everyone's patience is being tried at this point."

Then Pondurious, who appeared to marvel at the sincerity of the young human's conviction, addressed Darius's request. "Young Darius, in all my years, I have not yet met anyone with as much passion and conviction as you. You have shown this in the courage before those who are much older and who hold authority over much. You have been called to question by others the wisdom of your father taking a great risk in his reputation and yours. I never once thought that your actions came from disrespect or anything less than pure, innocent inquiry."

"Thank you, sir," replied the young man. "But please, sir, what is your decision?"

Pondurious smiled endearingly at Darius once again, then turned to address all in the assembly. "Mayor Fredrick and all friends gathered before me. If all would so agree, I would like to honor the request of this young man. I ask because of Darius's courage and his demonstration of such great honor given to the story of new life I shared with you all."

The gathering began to stir, concerned and contemplative. "What could it hurt, Mayor?" rang out one voice from the crowd.

Argon spoke over the murmuring to answer the person's question, "I think we've wasted enough of our time."

But the murmuring only continued. Another person shouted over the noise, "You have nothing, Argon! I vote we let the sage give it a try!"

Then the crowd erupted into a cheer, with others shouting, "Yes, Argon, you have nothing! We are desperate to try anything!"

Rorke, being drowned out by the insistence of the crowd noise, called out in a final desperate attempt, "This is absurd. How could this possibly make any difference at all?"

Then Ditimus, maybe for the first time ever, seemed to find his voice, shouting over the crowd, "Ladies, gentlemen, Mayor!" The crowd all drew silent. The scribe had shell-shocked the crowd with his mouse-that-roared-like-a-lion's voice. Realizing all eyes were now focused on him, including the shocked mayor's, he continued, "We are all at a loss for what to do about this desperate situation we find ourselves in. We have built this great town on the backs of many of our relatives and neighbors who have gone before us. It is no misunderstanding that the loss we all stand to suffer is great if we cannot fix this critical resource. We have been told by the researchers and developers that there is no other source of water close enough to use as an alternate. We have also been told by our scientist that to correct the source of the geological fault which has caused this catastrophe is beyond anything human resources can provide. We are now being told the reason for this tragic event is because we live in a world broken and fallen, by our own doing. We have tried to blame others, and now, according to this sage, we are all to blame. I see no other course of action but to allow the message of the sage to be proven true or false."

The bewildered mayor glanced at his now emboldened scribe, then back at the crowd. "Ahem, ahem." With his throat cleared and a slight crack in his voice, he bellowed to the awaiting crowd, "Friends of this great town. My *highly* trusted servant, Ditimus, has just proven to all of you why he is indeed my right-hand man." Ditimus gave the mayor a put-out look. "I think the consensus here is that we allow the sage, Pondurious, to proceed with the recommendation of Felix's son, Darius. Argon and Rorke, would you please call on the water plant engineer, Regis, to guide us to the test insertion point at the base of the well opening?" This was the place where the water technicians could deposit the small sample of the sand and gold left behind under the body of Gamgus.

"I would like to request that Darius be allowed to be with the group overseeing this task," said Pondurious.

"Yes, of course." The mayor nodded. "Rorke and Argon, please come with us. Felix, you may come with us also." Turning to the remaining townspeople, the mayor announced, "My fellow townspeople. It is impossible for all to be present so please wait outside until we have completed this task. I will rely on those I have selected to accompany me to witness and affirm what happens when we finish." The crowd began to disperse, following the entourage loosely as they migrated in the direction of the main entrance to my great filtration plant.

Chapter 15 - White Sand and Gold

The filtration plant built over me was a stone-and-brick structure with a front entrance leading to the offices of the management staff. The entourage met Regis, one of the maintenance engineers, in the foyer. The foyer connected to the hallway lined with offices and a single door at the end of the hall. Behind that door housed all the water treatment equipment and operations, which were needed to maintain and supply water to the town. When they entered the plant process floor through that door, they encountered the large containers for the filtration area. This room was the size of a small theater with an assembly of giant filter containers connected by large blue pipes entering them and leaving the room.

"This is quite the operation you have here," remarked Felix.

"This is only the small of it," said the maintenance engineer. "As you will soon see, the operation is complex and if you don't know what you are doing, a lot of people are going to be without water. Of course, notwithstanding, we are experiencing that very situation."

When they entered the next section, they noticed the great pumps all parked in a row. Normally they would be humming with a deep whirling noise of bearings and sparks releasing ozone. But today, and for months prior, they were motionless and cold. The great pipes which connected them were silent as well, devoid of the usual low swishing of the flow of racing water.

"We are about to enter the main processing room," announced Regis. They approached large, steel double doors, hosting small tempered glass observation windows. Regis took his plant key and opened the doors to allow the entourage to enter the other side.

The processing room was typically a symphony of industrial noises being played and fussed over by the workers. It was an impressive display of great wheel valves and pressure meters, which had been carefully attended to in order to help maintain its operation. Today, as it had been for some time, they were all turned to their closed positions and the meters read zero pressure. The great water plant had for so long felt like a warm, comforting shelter as it drew from me, serving to remind me of how important I was. I would often thank it for allowing me to serve so many. It made me grateful for the humans and the craftwork of their hands. But now it lay silent, motionless, and dead above me.

"Welcome, gentlemen," the head supervisor of the plant, Benjamin, said, intercepting the small group. Benjamin was the last man standing in all matters of the plant. Being the chief administrative representative, he had very little working knowledge of how everything worked, which often got in the way. "Hello, Regis, I see you were able to show our guests about the plant."

Regis, who often had disputes with Benjamin, saw him more as an obstacle to his work. "Yes, of course, Ben, it was my pleasure," he halfheartedly replied.

"Well, Regis, then would you be so kind as to allow me to join with you?"

With a subtle look of annoyance, Regis nodded and continued to lead the entourage in the direction of the service opening, directly above my entry point.

Now turning to face the mayor, Benjamin inquired, "I understand you have special business you would like to see to, Mayor Fredrick?"

The mayor, who was still uncertain if what had been decided was really a good idea, replied, "Why yes. Well, you see, um…"

"We would like access to the main entry point of the well," interjected Darius.

"Excuse me, young man?" replied Benjamin. "Fredrick, who is this making such an unusual and unqualified request?"

"Pardon me," the sage answered. "We are aware that you are only acting in the best interest of protecting the property. Let me assure you that we are here to help and nothing bad will come of it."

"And who is this unusual character, Mayor?" retorted Benjamin.

"Pay no mind to your concerns, Ben," said the mayor in an assuring tone. "This is official business on behalf of the people of this town. The sage, Pondurious, and young Darius are convinced they can help. Those who gathered today to represent the town's interest have all agreed to let them try."

"I've seen this so-called *sage* before. Are you sure you trust him, Fredrick? I have heard strange rumors about him."

"Yes, yes, of course, Benjamin. We are all aware of that, but after some deliberation and expressed consent of the townspeople, I believe we should allow it." The mayor added, "After all, it is the will of the people. We should let the sage try."

Having no more appeals, the plant supervisor nodded at Regis, sanctioning the act. Regis spun the hand release bolts to my access door. As he had been doing for months now, he retrieved a test card from the tool pouch he carried by his side. The test card contained small squares of different shades of reactive papers with identification marks for determining and detecting the contents in the water. It had a hole punched in it on the end. By using a fine twine he produced from his bag, he tied it to the hole in the card and dropped the tethered card down the opening of the service hatch. By then, the pressure of the pumps had been off for some time, so the gravity point of my water was hovering a few feet below the opening edge. When he retrieved the card, he noted aloud that most of the colors were opposite the original color and much darker than they used to be. He shook his head as if it were a shame and told the scribe, Ditimus, who was writing to report on behalf of the mayor and all surrounding him, that the reading was worse than ever.

My water had a foul smell and a slight dark-green tint. Seeing the pinched expressions on the faces of the small gathering as they reacted to the smell made me feel more broken and useless than I had ever felt before. Then Pondurious reached for the amulet around his neck, holding it in the palm of his hand. He spoke to the small crowd before him. "I thank Ram the perpetual for all things. His thoughts and words create and sustain all matter, and in great humility I now ask His will to be accomplished today." Then he opened the amulet, carefully revealing the contents inside. The sand contained in the amulet was a fine powder and white as snow. It was so white, the porcelain amulet appeared to be gray surrounding it. From the surface of the sand, one could see the gold sparkle from the small grains of gold, which were catching the ambient light and making small reflections dance on the sage's face.

Darius, who was standing next to the sage with his head fixed down at the open amulet, gazed, stunned and still, as the gold reflections also beamed on his face. "How unlike anything I have ever seen," he remarked. "The sand is not a powder. I can see it is a very fine grain, having the properties that would allow it to be poured out. The gold particles in the sand are even more spectacular and amazing. They each have geometrical facets that give them a multimirror, reflective quality. They are very small and vary in size, as if they were each crafted under a microscope. I find myself lost in wonderment as I would when I see snowflakes, each unique and miraculous." The young man was now realizing something beyond the natural in the content of the sand and gold. The very small amount the sage had in the amulet represented a craftsmanship that would take years to accomplish for even the small amount he possessed. If the sage's story was true, then the amount said to be in possession in the Primus Regions would be an impossibility to be made by human efforts. At the very least, it would be impractical, taking years to complete any substantial quantity.

Pondurious again smiled at the young man. "Dearest friend, Darius," he said in response. "You are just beginning to understand. The closer you look, you will find more assurance of what is true." The sage then made a motion for him to reach for the sand and gold. "Young Darius, would you please have the honor and take the smallest pinch and drop it into the service opening of the well?"

Then the young man named Darius, with a surprised but honored look on his face, reached reverently and carefully for a very tiny pinch of the mysterious white sand and gold. He looked up at Pondurious, who, with a smile on his face, then gave the young man a nod. Darius leaned over into the opening of the service point and lightly and deliberately released the small particles into the water below. Rubbing his fingers back and forth for a few seconds to make sure all was gone, he looked back up at the sage, who was still smiling and motioning him to step away from the access door. Pondurious then closed the amulet with the remaining sand and gold. The maintenance engineer closed the service hatch and spun the clamping bolts to shut and seal the access point.

"Young Darius, I have been on a journey to share the truth of the new perpetual world to come for many years. It is my deepest joy to find those who would join with me in this tremendous task. When I was young like you, I was also moved by the telling of the sacrifice of Gamgus by another sage such as me. Until today, I have only found one with such great trust and desire for the truth. This truth being known by the awakening discovered in the gift offering of Ram the perpetual. The *Mission* I am certain now, dwells in you. What I am about to ask of you I do not take lightly, and until now I have only asked it of one other."

"What are you asking of me, sir?" the young man curiously inquired.

The sage answered Darius, saying, "For many years I have sojourned from town to town, being called to offer insight and hope in the places where the darkness of the fallen steward still hides from sight. We now exist in the time for all to soon be made new in the perpetual realm of Ram. All those who are made in His image are given the opportunity to find their hearts in gratitude for His sacrifice. He will not command those He loves to come to desire and trust Him. They must find the path in their own will through seeking what was given by Him. The time of cosmic treason and the penalty of such has been overcome and the sentence has been lifted for all who would accept, live, and hope in Ram's pardon. I am inviting you to join with me to speak and witness this truth to all parts of your corner of the world."

"Now wait just a minute, Pondurious!" Felix erupted. "My son has committed to help me with my business. I have invested much time and resources to train him, and if he leaves, I will suffer a great loss."

"I understand, Felix," Pondurious replied. "It would be a very difficult choice, and it will not be without consequences either way. But I can only ask Darius, and in the end, it can only be his choice and not yours. I believe you are a fair man, and your desire would be to allow him freedom to choose his path."

Felix paused to ponder what the sage just said. He then turned to his young son. "Of course, son, it is up to you to decide if you wish to join with Pondurious."

Darius smiled at his father. Then he turned to face the sage and asked him this question: "Sir, what became of the other who you deemed worthy of joining you as your apprentice?"

The sage lowered his head, a sad expression on his face. "He was not willing to leave behind his family and all he had worked for to join with me."

Then the young man turned to his father. "Father, you know I love you and I know you love me. I also am mindful that mother is no longer with us, and sister and I are all you have now. But father…" The young man paused, tears beginning to stream from his eyes. "I cannot forsake this calling I am feeling in my heart."

"Son," Felix responded, his eyes now beginning to fill with tears as well. "I give you my deepest wishes and hope for great joy to be found wherever you go. If your future be found with Pondurious, then let it be that these very tears are of great joy. I wish you well on your way."

Then the sage lifted his head from the sad thought of the one who had rejected his prior invitation. "Felix, my deepest affection and gratitude I am feeling for you. I know that much of what I see in your son is because of the father you have been to him."

"Thank you, Pondurious," Felix replied. "Please see to his well-being."

The sage turned to the others and thanked them for their trust. He then said, "I must now leave, but I leave you with the hope of a restored, new life that will one day find its reach to all corners of the universe. I am taking Darius with me for my help in sharing this hope, anticipating that we will see you again."

The mayor understood that all the sage could do was done and graciously thanked him. "When might we see you and Darius again, Pondurious?"

"Yes, Pondurious," echoed Felix, who was now beginning to anticipate the loss of his son. "I would like to know."

"I do not know the day or time, but I do know that his return is meant to be," the sage assured the mayor, Felix, and the others surrounding them. When they left the great filtration plant, the gathering of humans who were waiting outside greeted them. Some wanted to question them, while others of the town took turns shaking the sage's hand and wishing him well on his journey back to the others like him.

Rorke did not wish them well. "I cannot see how any of this will make any difference," he said to Argon under his breath.

"We are still just as bad off and it is likely we solved nothing," Argon responded. "Such a waste of our time if you ask me. Nothing other than wishful thinking and so unscientific." But out of respect for the sage's time, they both reluctantly shook his hand and halfheartedly wished him well. I was uncertain and had doubts. I was once again feeling toxic, empty, and useless. Then everyone went their separate ways to return to their homes, leaving the human maintenance workers to keep watch at the plant.

As the sage and young man were leaving the gathering to prepare for departure, I couldn't help but ponder their conversation. "Young Darius, we will say a final farewell to your father and sister as you collect the essentials for the journey that awaits us."

"Yes, sir," replied the young man. "What should I bring with me?"

Pondurious replied, "We will be on foot for many miles, and will need to charter a ship to sail from the east coast to the west. We will trust Ram to provide all our needs. You will need one change of clothes, a coat for cold nights, and two blankets. One blanket to sleep on and one to cover you."

"Yes, sir. Where are we going?" Darius questioned with a concerned tone and expression.

"Worry not, my dear friend," answered the sage, smiling at Darius. "We are going to set our sights on returning to the area once called the Primus Regions, where you will meet the people I come from. Much may happen along the way, but please, you may call me by my name. I will teach you much and we will be on a first-name basis."

"Yes, of course, Pondurious, sir," the young man awkwardly replied.

Pondurious smiled and asked him a most curious question. "Darius, do you believe that the water of the well will be restored?"

"Yes, if Ram wills it," the young man replied.

"Do you believe it is Ram's will?" continued the sage.

"Yes, I do," said the young man. "I have no doubt of it."

"Why do you have no doubt, Darius?" inquired the sage.

Darius paused for a moment to think about the question. "Pondurious, sir." The young man was still uncomfortable addressing the sage by his first name. "You have shown me that it is indeed the will of Ram the perpetual that all will one day be restored to a perpetual existence, so even if it is not accomplished in my lifetime, it does not mean it will not be done. You have also shown me that much work is still to be done to prepare for that final Day of Reconciliation. It certainly can't be for me to know when or where all things will be performed."

The sage gave him a beaming smile. "Darius, my dear friend, you have shown me great faith and understanding. I am so renewed with hope, strength, and encouragement. Thank you."

"But, sir...I mean, Pondurious, uh, sir." The young man was taken aback by such a humble thank you from one he looked up to. "How is it possible that I, being so new in understanding, could possibly give you so much?"

Pondurious, still smiling at the young man, asked him another most puzzling question, "Darius, my dear friend. Is it the sand and gold that will perform the restoration of the water in the well?"

Darius was silent for a moment as he pondered the sage's question. "Sir, I mean, Pondurious. I do not think it will be the sand and gold. Even though it possessed such unusual and, one might even say, *supernatural* properties."

Pondurious was now looking at the young man with intrigue. "So for what reason should we commit the sand and gold to the water? Is it not enough to just believe Ram would do it?"

Once again, Darius paused to think. After a longer and more thoughtful period had expired, he answered. "Most respectfully Pondurious. You have shown me that Ram includes the physical for our sake. The sand and gold are truly a remarkable thing. It demonstrates the physical of the nature of Ram. But it is still only a *thing* and not who Ram is. The fact that only a very small amount of the sand and gold exist on the planet shows me that it is very precious and rare. I believe it was for our sake that Ram reminds us that something so small as a pinch of the sand and gold shows us that even someone so small as one human holding just a pinch of real faith in Ram possesses great power."

The sage put his arm around the young man, obviously approving of his answer. "Yes, young Darius. But you miss one point. Ram only ever wanted your desire and trust in Him. You are not very small in His sight. In fact, He gave everything so you would come to find yourself where you are right now." And with those words, they left together.

Chapter 16 - The Wish of the Well

The next morning, the filtration plant worker named Mannion arrived to do the usual inspection of the facility. One of his duties was making sure nothing was disturbed by those who may wish to cause harm to the plant. I have been untapped for a long time now. This made the plant building still and dead, subjecting it to mischief from vandals. He would also do certain monitoring and testing to observe any more changes to my situation. He was not aware of what the sage and the young man had done. The treatment of the sand and gold had happened when he was off shift and at home. Casually and routinely, it was time to check the status of my water. He retrieved a test card and twine, then opened the service opening to perform a water sample analysis. He leaned over into the service opening and lowered the card into the water with the twine attached. Retrieving the card, he studied the results. What he saw caused him to rub and then squint his eyes, as if not believing what he saw there. All the reactive squares on the card indicated a perfect water sample! He felt the card, presumably to make sure it was wet and had been submerged. Much to his surprise, the card was indeed wet. He reached for a new, dry one, obviously thinking the first must have been defective, and repeated the test, making sure he could see that the card was submerged. Looking down through the service opening, he could see it floating on the water like a leaf on a pond. He waited a longer time than usual, just to make sure the card had a good chance of exposure. When he pulled the card up, he was gobsmacked. The card, much to his amazement, indicated the same results. "This cannot be right!" the plant worker said out loud.

"What is going on, Mannion?" said Regis. He was just arriving for work and noticed his associate bustling at my service opening.

Mannion showed his coworker the card reading. "That can't be right." In the past, when my water was drinkable, there were usually slight changes in some of the squares, but never had the card come up completely perfect. Regis leaned over into the service opening and took a deep breath to see if the foul smell was still present, and much to his surprise, he couldn't smell any hint of an offensive odor. He grabbed a test flask from a workbench and lowered it into me to draw out a sample. When he retrieved the sample, he found it to be perfectly clear. The green tint was gone. The water was crystal clear, turning the flask into a magnifying device. At this point they were both at a loss for words. Grabbing the exposed test card and flask filled with my water sample, they both made haste to the plant supervisor.

Almost out of breath, the plant workers arrived at the supervisor's office. "What is this all about, gentlemen?" Benjamin asked, sitting in his chair with his legs propped up on his desk. He was sipping from his morning drink in one hand while reading a book with the other. He couldn't help but notice them both slightly frazzled.

Catching his breath, Regis replied, "You are not going to believe what we just discovered, Ben."

The plant supervisor retorted, "Well, don't make me guess. Out with it." He sat up in his chair, setting his book and drink on the desk.

Mannion cut in on Regis before he could reply. "You are not going to believe the readings we just took on the water inlet access, Ben!"

"Let me guess, Mannion…worse than ever," the supervisor said with annoyance.

"Not exactly." Regis held forward the flask of crystal-clear water.

"What is the meaning of this, Regis?" It was obvious he was upset that his morning solitude was interrupted.

Mannion answered ahead of Regis, anxious to break the news first. "This is the most current sample of the water from the well, post entry point."

"Is this some kind of joke? Just yesterday the water had a dark color and a foul odor. Am I to really believe this came from the same well? If you are trying to get one over on me, then you picked a bad time to interrupt my much-needed time of solace."

"This is no joke, Ben," Regis said. He then retrieved the last test card reading from the well from his shirt pocket and handed it to the annoyed plant supervisor.

"You can't be serious, Regis. This can't be true," said the supervisor, now seeing a perfect test card.

"We're sorry we interrupted your special time, Ben; you really *do* need to come with us and see for yourself," said Regis.

"Well, all right then. This is going to be a good one," the supervisor replied sarcastically. Slowly standing up, he followed the two plant workers on their course towards my opening.

When the three plant workers arrived at my access point, Benjamin took matters into his own hands. "Let's see what this is all about. Please hand me a test card, Regis." Regis tied a length of twine to a test card and handed it to the plant supervisor. He lowered it into the opening and waited a minute. Then he raised it to see what it read, studying it with an intense expression on his face. He then turned his head towards the plant workers. "This is impossible, gentlemen," he said, still doubting what he was seeing with his own eyes. "Are you certain you haven't got a batch of defective cards, Regis?"

"These were from the same lot that showed the contamination just yesterday, Ben," Regis assured him.

"Hand me a flask, Mannion," the supervisor commanded. He was given the flask and lowered it down to fill it up with some of my water. When he brought it to the surface and held it to the light, he saw for himself that my water was perfectly clear. Taking turns looking back and forth at the two plant workers with a bewildered expression, he smelled the water. "It has a slightly sweet smell to it. If I didn't know any better, I'd say it smells like honeysuckle." Much to the objection of the plant workers, the plant supervisor, with a cautious but curious expression, touched the water with the tip of his tongue. There was no sense of reaction on his tongue, so he decided to take a very small, cautious sip of the water. Closing his eyes, he slowly tipped the opening of the flask towards his lips and drank a very small amount. His eyes flew open. He had a satisfied smile on his face, as if he was experiencing what he had never felt before. A perfect refreshing sensation followed by a sense of well-being. It was as if the water contained properties so pure it offered no offense but only refreshment and revival. "This water is the purest and sweetest-tasting I have ever experienced. It is not even the same as it was when the well was *not* contaminated. It now possesses an amazing quality that makes it divine!"

The two plant workers exchanged glances, then each took turns tasting my restored water.

"This water is amazing!" Mannion exclaimed.

"I can't believe what I am tasting. How is this possible?" remarked Regis.

"In any case, Regis," replied Benjamin, "we need to call the mayor to discuss and *try* to explain our findings. As hard as it is to believe, and as impossible as it may be, he still needs to be the first to know."

Soon the mayor and his faithful scribe, Ditimus, arrived at the plant to meet the plant supervisor and all who were waiting. "What is this all about, Ben?" the mayor said to the plant supervisor. Ditimus stood by his side, ready and poised to record all the events that were about to take place.

"An extraordinary course of events has unfolded, Fred," the plant supervisor answered the mayor. Ditimus was now scribbling, taking notes in his record book while the plant supervisor explained everything to the mayor.

"This is most incredible, Ben, but I am having a very hard time believing what you say is true." After the mayor heard the testimony of the plant supervisor and the plant engineer showed him the evidence, he said, "I am hesitant to show any hope and excitement over your findings. I think we should call on our scientists and researchers and developers to sanction these findings."

"I would wholeheartedly agree, Fred. The sooner the better," replied the plant supervisor.

Immediately, they summoned Argon and Rorke. They were soon all gathered at my service opening. They each took turns confirming the test cards and tasting the water.

Argon brought with him his microscope and other test gear. "I cannot scientifically explain what my results show," he said, shaking his head, and for the first time in his life, having doubt in his voice. "My readings show that this water is free from any contaminants. No signs of harmful parasites or microorganisms are present. The water from this well prior to its contamination contained such particles. This justified our filters and chemicals we needed to add to keep the water safe for human consumption." The scientist looked down once again into his microscope, then looked back up at the other humans gathered and said, "Remarkable."

Rorke had very few words for what he was experiencing. "I have come to trust the science, and as much as it seems impossible, the science proves this water appears to be safe to drink. If anything, it is safer than it has ever been."

"I would like to add one thing to the findings," Argon offered. "This water contains a strange and unrecognizable particle that I can't explain. Perhaps it is what gives it the unusual, sweet smell."

"This information troubles me," said the plant engineer. If it can't be explained, then perhaps we should try to filter it out in case it is found to be harmful.

"Yes, Regis, one can't be too safe. Can you see if it is possible?" replied the mayor.

"In your best guess, Argon, what would you say is the average particle size of this substance you are observing?" inquired Regis.

"Based on my magnification settings, I would say between five to point two five microns would be a good range to try," answered Argon.

The mystery of my new water continued. Using many test filters, the plant maintenance worker and the plant engineer made attempt after attempt to filter the unexplained particles out of my water. They tried filter range after filter range, and yet, the particles were still present. They even added particles that were the same visual size as the foreign ones, only to see those added removed with the filters and the mystery ones remaining.

"I just can't explain this," the now frustrated Argon said. "It is as if they *are* but are *not* there."

"Now you're beginning to sound like that sage, Argon," interjected Rorke with a cutting, satirical chuckle. The scientist looked up once again from his microscope and gave him a nasty, defiant look.

"Enough, gentlemen!" the mayor barked. "We have been here for hours now. It appears we can't explain this phenomenon. I only need to know, is the water safe or not?"

"None of us can make that assurance, Fred," said the plant supervisor. "It would take weeks, if not months, to run studies to conclude that. But the final decision will ultimately be yours. I'm not sure that there wouldn't be some kind of revolt if the word got out that the water only had one questionable flaw. People might be willing to take a chance anyway."

The mayor found himself in a predicament. Should he face more pressure by waiting? Should he disclose the flaw and leave it to a vote, or not disclose the flaw and take the chance that people would be harmed, or helped, if he sanctioned the water? The mayor turned to his scribe. "What do you think I should do, Ditimus?"

The scribe Ditimus stopped his writing. The mayor had asked his opinion many times in the past, only to reject them. Why should he bother now? But Ditimus was loyal to the mayor, and he said something surprising and unexpected. "It appears to me, sir, that the very reason for the change in the water was a result of the sand and gold, while believing in something hoped for. The result of that hope being played out in action *did* produce the result we see today. I see no reason why you shouldn't follow through by deciding based on believing the water is safe."

"Are you saying if I believe the water is safe, then it will be?" the mayor replied to Ditimus. "Isn't that just the same as taking a chance? What if I am wrong and people are hurt?"

Ditimus, now finding the legs of great, unexpected wisdom, answered the mayor, "It would be taking a chance if you didn't have all the facts before you. But you do have the facts, which state that the impossible has already happened. No one will fault you if this was enough for you to take a leap of faith and make the decision because you believe it is the right thing to do."

"So, mayor," inserted Rorke, "do you believe it is the right thing to sanction the use of the water and take the responsibility for the results?"

For the first time in the mayor's political career, he was forced to decide based on what he believed and not what would be safe or popular. Then, probably for the first time in his life, it was clear that a feeling of confidence rose up within his chest and the conviction of his belief became his guide, because he said, "I believe the water is safe to drink. In fact, I think I believe that it is more than safe to drink. Ben, we will meet with the town right away and announce the reopening of the plant."

"I will set to task the work of recommissioning the plant, Fred," replied the plant supervisor.

The plant workers began to work with the scientist to determine what filters were needed to make it suitable for mass consumption. I could feel the cool and crisp sensation of my water leaving me as they drew more and more samples. Chemical analysis determined the water was rich with most, if not all, the minerals which had been supplemented previously by the filters and additive chambers. It was determined the only filter needed was the safety check filter, which would be used if there were any sediment-type elements, which in the past would appear from time to time. But to everyone's amazement, all the filters and additive chambers were now set to bypass the water flowing through them. They all worked around the clock to ready the towers to be flushed with the new water and then filled to be released to the town.

The great red pumps began to come back to life with a low hum, and the sparking of the windings and brushes produced a smell of hot bearings and ozone. Soon the water from my source was racing through the pipes in the rooms of the plant and filling the great water towers. Mayor Fredrick ordered all his staff and the communication agencies to contact all the townspeople to meet at the gazebo in front of me for a special announcement.

When the humans were gathered, there was much chatter, and the crowd was a low rumble of voices, awaiting the special announcement from the mayor. The town facility workers set up the now needed amplification system so the speeches from the gazebo could be heard by everyone attending the assembly. Then the mayor stepped to the microphone and began to speak, "Citizens of this great town, it is with great joy that I announce to everyone that our water crisis has been solved!" The crowd erupted in cheering and applause, then became quiet at the mayor's motion to settle down. He continued once he had everyone's attention. "A great work has been done to restore our water supply. A work which has saved this town and all its industry from being laid waste. This morning, the supervisor of this great filtration plant, our research and development staff, *and* our most distinguished scientists give me confidence to confirm our water is not only safe to drink but is now beyond the quality of anything we have ever experienced, both near and far." The crowd erupted in applause and cheering again while the mayor stood proud, offering a smile of political elation. He then continued when the applause died down, "I would like to thank all involved in this, for lack of a better word, *miraculous* feat. For starters, I would like to invite our esteemed representative of the research and development team, Rorke Kamilton, to share some words about how all of this was made possible."

The crowd began to cheer for Rorke, only to see him making a gesture of refusal and an embarrassed head shake.

The mayor quickly jumped in. "Well, oh, it appears he is at a loss for words, so then I give you our very own head scientist from the esteemed science department, Argon Muchinelli!"

Argon nervously stepped up to the podium. "Uh, thank you, Mayor Fredrick. Well, uh, you see…" He cleared his throat and continued after an awkward pause, "Science has for so long been about the facts that present themselves coupled with statistical analysis. When such events are presented in such a hypothesis as this, well, one could only conclude that the inevitable should occur, naturally."

The crowd was now brought to a perplexed pause of silence. Then one of the spectators broke the silence and shouted out, "Spoken like a true scientist, Argon!" Looking around at the surrounding crowd, he added, "Can someone explain to me what he just said?"

Then the crowd erupted in laughter. Argon's countenance went from awkward to condescending. "I'm sorry I can't explain it more simply," he retorted with a contemptible tone.

The mayor, trying to quell the crowd's ridicule, took the microphone from Argon. "Please, please, everyone. Let us be respectful of one so dedicated to the sciences." The crowd settled. "It is quite alright, Argon. Most people do not spend as much time with beakers and test tubes like you do." This public validation was meant to be a compliment. Unfortunately, the mayor was just as confounded by Argon's words, so his public acknowledgement of the talents of Argon only caused the crowd to erupt in laughter again. Argon gave the mayor a subtle sneer and returned to his seat.

By now, the crowd noticed the mayor's first choices to give account were not able to answer and an awkward silence fell over the gathering. The mayor cleared his throat, which now reverberated to the buildings behind the crowd. "Ahem, perhaps our head supervisor of the filtration plant, Benjamin, could express it in layman's terms?"

Benjamin sheepishly approached the podium, and with a quiet and untrained voice, he deferred, "I have witnessed events that I cannot, with great confidence, relay to everyone gathered. But there is one among us who I know kept good account and should be called upon to reliably play back the course of events."

Then the mayor whispered at Benjamin, hiding his mouth with his hand, "Who might that be, Ben?"

The plant supervisor continued, "I believe there is one among us who has shown the capacity to bring an honest recollection of what has happened. I would like to call to your attention the mayor's scribe, Ditimus."

The crowd then became silent. After an awkward pause, a low murmuring began to slowly rise among the gathering. Ditimus had a stunned and fearful expression on his face for being called out into the light of public discourse. He had always been in the shadow of the mayor. But today he was being called to address a crowd that he only comfortably faced hiding *behind* the mayor. He slowly approached the microphone, and when he was in front of it, he looked down at his record book.

"Are you sure about this, Ben?" whispered the mayor. Benjamin gave a quick nod of approval.

Ditimus then looked up from his record book. It was as if he suddenly realized something from everything he had witnessed and recorded. Once again, Ditimus found his legs in wisdom. He cleared his throat, and the crowd once again became silent to give the quiet voice room to be heard. "Many of you are familiar with the story told by the sage, Pondurious, when asked to explain why our well had become contaminated." Seeing he now had everyone's undivided attention, Ditimus continued, "Pondurious spoke of a great new beginning of everything which is and will be. He said Ram the perpetual, who is the three persons of the *Why*, *Reason*, and the *Mission*, had always intended all matter of the universe to one day be reconciled to His perpetual existence. Until He allowed the perfect sacrifice, a human who was His Son, the *Reason*, sent, all laid waste to His law of entropy, where all was moving towards atrophy and death. This state of existence was why the well became poisoned and all hope was lost for restoration. But the great hope in those troubled waters was Ram's work accomplished in the great cathedral of Myrobah. This work proves all is under Ram's dominion. His will being established in the hearts of humanity by being courted back to Himself. This gift given to this town by His wonderful act of grace was allowed to happen so you might know this truth."

Then something mysterious and wonderful began to happen. The crowd began to make a strange but wonderful sound. It was the sound of those beginning to cry. It was not the sound of desperate sobbing, as if all was lost, but rather wails of joy, as if a great tsunami of gratitude was approaching. Many of the humans began to cry out thanks to Ram the perpetual. Then Ditimus was at a loss for more to say and slowly stepped back. The wondrous sound of joyful gratitude filled the courtyard for what seemed like a never-ending chorus.

When the crowd began to settle, Mayor Fredrick, who also had red, tear-soaked eyes, stepped up to the podium. The tone of his speech was not with the political bravado he started with but was now quiet, subdued, and peaceful. He thanked his loyal scribe Ditimus for his wonderful spiritual insight and then asked Benjamin to come to the podium for departing instructions.

"My friends of this great town," Benjamin opened with. "Please return to your homes and places of business to open water supply valves, allowing the old water left in them to purge out. When you begin to smell a very faint fragrance of honeysuckle, you will know the water is now safe to drink." When the assembly was over, the townspeople returned to their homes to follow the instructions of the plant supervisor.

In the following days, the town noticed the benefit from me. The faces of the townspeople looked brighter, and the attitudes towards each other began to change. Before, they were quiet and for the most part kept to themselves. Now, they were becoming more cheerful and helpful towards each other.

They gathered at the gazebo before me on a regular schedule to sing joyful songs about the perpetual new world Ram was to bring to all who desire and trust Him. They shared together the tradition of the last meal with Gamgus as was introduced by the sage, Pondurious and later suggested by Ditimus. My water is celebrated, possessing qualities that renew the physical health of the humans. Above all, it serves to remind all who drink it of the hope in a promise yet to be fully realized.

I now know there are no mistakes or events which happen without a purpose and meaning. Although some events may be seen as a great catastrophe, from such, Ram brings forth the opportunity to remind us we are powerless over most all things. But the one thing we are not powerless over is the choice we make in who and what we trust in and desire. Before us, He brings us either the opportunity to trust Him in the trials of a fallen world being brought to renewal or the opportunity to see His redeeming power delivering us from them. Each is just as important, allowing all to walk in and with the person of the *Mission*. Everyone, without His help, is cut off from all the goodness His coming perpetual existence brings. All those who live in the finished work of Gamgus have now been given the *Mission* in hope and the promise of being restored to the perpetual realm of Ram. May this hope present itself to all, for it is truly Ram's will that all would come to Him.

I am the Well, placed and established with precision and care. I now know where I am is where I need to be. All the water flowing from my depths now offers to all who drink from me the reminder and assurance of the perpetual life to come.

More will be revealed.

Made in the USA
Middletown, DE
22 January 2026